PIRATING PUPS:
SALTY SEA-DOGS
AND
BARKING BUCCANEERS

PIRATING PUPS:
SALTY SEA-DOGS
AND
BARKING BUCCANEERS

EDITED BY
RHŌNDA PARRISH

TYCHE BOOKS LTD.

Pirating Pups: Salty Sea-Dogs and Barking Buccaneers
Edited by Rhonda Parrish
Copyright © 2022

Published by Tyche Books Ltd.
Calgary, Alberta, Canada
www.TycheBooks.com

Cover Art by Sarah Dahlinger
Cover Layout by Indigo Chick Designs
Interior Layout by Ryah Deines
Editorial by Rhonda Parrish

First Tyche Books Ltd Edition 2022
This Edition 2024
Print ISBN: 978-1-989407-79-0
Ebook ISBN: 978-1-989407-48-6

Author photograph: Cindy Gannon Photography

This book was funded in part by a grant from the Alberta Media Fund.

Alberta
Government

CONTENTS

Introduction — Rhonda Parrish 1

The Empress of Marshmallow — Chadwick Ginther 3

Davy Bones and the Domestication of the Dutchman —
Jennifer Lee Rossman 21

Johnson the Terror — Meghan Beaudry.................... 29

Ghost Pirate Dognapper — Kristen Brand 37

Blackbark's Collar — Richard Lau 47

Let the Water Drink First — V.F. LeSann 53

New Tricks — Alice Dryden 73

Torvi, Viking Queen — Melanie Marttila 87

Under the Curse of Jupiter — Mathew Austin............ 93

The Boomer Bust — JB Riley 113

What Gold Smells Like — Frances Pauli.................. 123

Artistic Appropriation — George Jacobs 143

What Frisky Wrought When the Wheels Fell Off the

World — E.C. Bell 149

Biographies 169

Does the Dog Die? — Rhonda Parrish 175

Dedicated to dogs.
All dogs.
Because they are the goodest.

. . . and to Jo. Who is also amazing.

Introduction

Rhonda Parrish

A COUPLE YEARS ago a Twitter conversation inspired the *Swashbuckling Cats: Nine Lives on the Seven Seas* anthology. Very early on in the process I started joking about how if the pirate cats anthology was successful I wanted to do a dog-centric sequel. It was a long shot at best, though. How successful could an anthology of pirate cat stories really be, after all?

And then I put the anthology together and found that the answer as, "Actually, really damn good." So then I turned up the half jokes about how I was going to do a dog-centric sequel. But not with a whole lot of intention behind it because there was so much going on in the world and my planner already, and was Tyche Books actually going to be interested in taking a chance on another super niche anthology in the middle of a pandemic? Who knew . . .

And then *Swashbuckling Cats* and one of the stories within it both got nominated for an Aurora award. And then "All Cats Go to Valhalla" by Chadwick Ginther won the Aurora award for best short story.

I believe the conversation* with Margaret from Tyche Books went something like, "So, are we doing this?"

"Yeah, let's do this!"

And so now I'm excited to share this anthology of sea-faring pups with you.

I made an error with *Swashbuckling Cats* that I do not want to repeat with *Pirating Pups*, though, so this anthology comes with a warning. Bad things do occasionally happen to dogs in this book. When those things happen, they are usually off the page and sort of waved or hinted at rather than described, but they do happen.

If you want to read with no spoilers, proceed as usual. However, for this anthology's version of "Does the dog die?" consult the back of the book where I've included a list of each story and what bad things happen to the puppers so you can decide which stories you want to read and which to avoid.

I hope this will help people experience the anthology without having to be on the edge of your seat in a bad way.

Enjoy!

Rhonda
Edmonton
2/23/22

* Time is weird and I don't remember if we had the conversation before the Auroras or after but . . . for simplicity's sake let's just *pretend* it was after. It makes for better flow in the story I'm telling here. :-p

THE EMPRESS OF MARSHMALLOW

CHADWICK GINTHER

THE EMPRESS OF Marshmallow surveyed her lakeside protectorate, maintained eye contact with the Thing in the Lake, and slowly, purposefully, shit on the beach.

She could see the Thing. A shimmering mirage. A daub of darkness against the sky. Its smell stretched, seemingly infinitely, from horizon to water's edge. The giant serpent, a car-length in diameter, trembled with anticipation at the packed beach. Its wedge-shaped, frilled maw hung over the sands, but it never broke the threshold of the lapping waves, as if a powerful barrier kept it at bay. This same barrier kept her human subjects from panicking like rabbits. The Empress chuffed a soft bark, and kicked up sand behind her.

The Boy Who Mattered, who most of her subjects called "Will," finally noticed The Empress's dominance. "Aw, Marshmallow, not on the beach!"

Ignoring the Boy's cries, and his disrespectful public omission of her title, the Empress maintained her locked gaze with the Thing. The Boy's lot was to clean up after her. It was *hers* to keep him safe. She would watch the Thing in the Lake until it slithered back beyond the horizon. She growled again, curled tail straightening and cream-coloured fur stiffening.

3

The Girl Who Almost Belonged, "Tilda," stiffened too, and not at the Empress's growls. The Girl didn't fear the Empress—which the Empress did not care for—but usually respected her place in court (unlike the Boy's mother). The Empress chanced looking away from the Thing to glance at the Girl. She, too, stared at the lake, and the Thing within.

It hadn't moved. It was still contained by her domain's magical protections.

Straight vertical and horizontal scratches in reality ringed the harbour like a fence. The scratches smelled of lightning, blood, and the salt of hard labour on a hot day. They glowed to the Empress, bright enough it amazed her none of the humans noticed. They were heedless to scents and many other treasures and dangers, so she wasn't surprised.

The work itself, intricate slices of power, were almost a language she could hear in her mind, as if their secrets were constantly being whispered. A warning so comprehensive, no monster would dare intrude. Warnings alone were nothing without the power to back them up, and the Empress knew that power was within her. It had to be, for was she not the ruler here? The Thing dared not face her in her domain. She barked again, growling at the tide.

The Thing in the Lake gradually submerged, its stink mostly hidden by water and fish, and its body by the foaming waves.

Still got it.

GIMLI WAS A beachside resort town an hour from Winnipeg. The times and place names meant nothing to The Empress of Marshmallow, but she knew the sounds and had ascribed them meaning. Gimli was her court's home. "Winnipeg" meant a *car ride*, either being primped at her groomers or the indignation of a visit to the veterinarian. Her attendants always tried to confuse her about the travel's purpose, to use the excitement of "car ride" to befuddle her. Sometimes they said they were going to one and arrived at the other. Or worse, both. The Empress was now mistrustful of both servants. Clearly, the groomer worked in cahoots with the veterinarian to befuddle her.

Winnipeg, and all people with its scent, were suspicious. Their presence increased through the summer, culminating now in the heat of August. The Great Destruction was coming—a festival. It brought street vendors, parades, crowded streets full with too many people from Winnipeg (and elsewhere), loud music (So! Much! Noise!) but *so many* smells (and other dogs). Enough, almost, to hide even the Thing in the Lake.

Almost.

The Thing in the Lake would never hide from the Empress of Marshmallow.

Many people lived in her community. She only cared for three: The Foodbringer (Sean), his son, The Boy Who Mattered, and the Boy's best friend, The Girl Who Almost Belonged. It was unusual for a chow chow to bond with someone outside the family unit, but the children were together so frequently, she'd become like one of the household. Besides, the Empress of Marshmallow didn't care for the Boy's mother, Agnes Who Didn't Care for Dogs. The woman balked at her court's every necessary expense, fed her nothing from their table, and had *banished her from the couch*.

As if she had the power.

Too many people believed they had the right to paw their Empress. To speak to her as if she wanted to hear their words. Her cream colouring, curled tail, and teddy bear face made everyone want to pet her, and she *did not want that*. She had a reputation to maintain as a fierce and mercurial ruler.

The children walked to the nearest bin to dispose her waste. This irked the Empress, as she'd left it where she'd intended, a reminder to the Thing in the Lake of who ruled in Gimli, but the Boy meant well.

"There was supposed to be a replica longship at the festival this year," the Boy said, kicking a stone down the path.

"So?"

"Owner's a no-show. There's just some crummy York boat." He stuck his tongue out toward the harbour.

"Vikings, Vikings, Vikings," the Girl said, truth buried in her teasing tone. "That's all you ever talk about, Will."

He smiled. "Isn't that the whole point of this town?"

"There's more to it than that," she said.

"Like what?"

Her response was a conspiratorial whisper. "It's a secret."

"Spill."

She looked to the inland sea. To the dirt. Scuffed a shoe.

Tossed a rock. "I'm not supposed to."

"Yeah, right. Secret."

"It's true. Amma would skin me."

"Bullshit." The Boy checked if any adults nearby heard the profanity. The Empress heard such words from him all the time. Safe from adult supervision, he repeated the profanity. "*Total* bullshit. Your grandma loves you. Thinks the sun shines out of your butt."

"She has a funny way of showing it sometimes. She even bullies my *mom*. Sometimes I want to run away and never come back. It would be easier."

"Where would that leave me?" The Empress sensed his worry. The girl was the only true friend her charge had. She drew closer so the Boy could scratch behind her ears. A small reward he accepted with grace. She made a happy chuffing sound, and he smiled faintly.

The Girl noticed the smile. "You really want to sail on a boat?"

"I want an adventure. A *viking* boat."

"A *viking* boat." The Empress could tell the Girl had moderated her tone, biting back her typical snark. "I'll get you an adventure. C'mon."

The Girl dragged the Boy toward the water, and the Empress of Marshmallow ran after. A ruler had to keep her subjects safe.

There were monsters in that lake.

AN OVAL OF head-sized stones stood out from a manicured grass field overlooking the harbour. Its sharp pinched edges on either end evoked the outline of a boat large enough for two adult humans to lie in side by side. The Empress sniffed around the perimeter. Other dogs had been by. Youthful drinkers. The Girl's scent was especially strong here. The Empress marked the closest rock. A reminder. This too, was hers, and the scents should tell that tale.

In the distance, the busy work setting up the Viking Village for the tourists was complete. The smells there were far more intriguing to the Empress: people in tents, cooking over open fires, who stank of metal and sweat for the Great Destruction's duration.

"Get in," the Girl insisted. "We're going sailing."

The Boy looked at the rocks, at her, back at the rocks. "You're crackers."

"I *said*, get in."

The Boy exaggeratedly stepped into the rock outline boat, as if he were carefully crossing the gunwales of a real boat, and sat in the centre. "Don't want to 'rock' it," he sneered, laughing uncontrollably.

Neither the Empress or the Girl appreciated his jest.

"C'mon, girl," the Girl said to the Empress, coaxing with her fingers.

Girl, indeed. She growled and dug in her heels, tugging on her lead.

"Marshmallow, Marshmallow," the girl teased. "Afraid of the water."

Afraid of the water. *Afraid*. The Empress of Marshmallow feared nothing. It wasn't the water which *concerned* her. She knew what was in the lake. The Girl had seen it too, and should know better. It was not the water keeping her away. On a hot day, it brought relief, certainly, but it also brought pain. Water could get trapped in her thick undercoat, and cause unseemly sores. And the smell. *The Smell*. The lake reek would cling to her coat for days, but she had sworn to protect the Boy from his own foolishness.

The Boy was a puppy who hadn't learned to use all his senses yet. If he couldn't see the Thing in the Lake, couldn't even smell it, then he couldn't protect himself, and it fell to the Empress to do it correctly. The Empress dug in her paws against her lead, backing away from the rocks. The Boy knew not to drag her somewhere she didn't want to be. If he tried, she'd slip her lead and run. He had a hard time catching her in a fenced yard. In the open, like this field, *impossible*.

Another tug. The Boy pleaded, "Marshmallow, c'mon."

The Empress's disdain was palpable. The Girl stared, as if looking through her, no, into her, and her scent became sharp, and bright as the wards.

"Your Highness," Tilda said gravely, finally using the appropriate amount of deference, "we will be doing this. With the Empress of Marshmallow's approval or without. But we would prefer to have her blessing. And her protection."

The Boy sighed, as he always did, when the proper forms were observed. Strange how the Girl always knew what to say, and how to say it, to calm the Empress's ire. She had no ruler, and yet, she knew.

The Girl waited for the Empress to acknowledge her. Which she did, allowing a quick scratch behind the ears. The Girl had addressed the Empress with respect, and should be rewarded. The Empress barked once, irritated, and lowered her curled tail to transmit her displeasure to her charge.

She sniffed to the inland sea—the Thing was closer than normal. But this "boat" was one in shape and name only. They were still on land. The Boy was still safe in the Empress's domain. She hopped nimbly over the stones and sat beside him.

"Pleased to have you." The Girl drew a small, weathered stone from her pocket, rubbing it between her thumb and forefingers, eyes closed. "You're the one who wants to go sailing. I need something from you to make your adventure happen."

The Boy's eyes narrowed. Those words *always* got him in trouble.

"What?"

"Spit on the rocks."

"*What?*"

"Piss would work too."

He looked around. "Someone will see."

"No one wants to see your wiener."

"Obviously *you* do."

"I've seen it," she reminded him. "Once was enough."

"*Fine.* I'll *spit* on the rocks."

He did. The Girl spread the saliva like painting a canvas, and after tearing up bits of grass, drew upon the rocks with dirt.

"You're touching my spit."

"Don't be gross."

"*You're* gross. You wanted to touch my pee."

The Girl didn't respond, and the Empress knew she'd allowed the Boy to believe he'd won the exchange, while she concentrated on her work. The Girl traced a symbol on each stone in turn. She whispered a word the Empress had never heard. "Naudhiz."

"What did you say?"

"It's a rune. The need-rune," she said. "It's *my* rune."

"Runes. *Vikings.*" He nodded, as if things were *finally* on track. The Girl continued drawing her shapes upon the stones. "Your weird family and their mumbo jumbo fortune-telling is finally paying off."

"We tell anyone who'll listen, and will pay our price, but nobody thinks what we tell them is 'fortune.'"

"Mom called you all a bunch of grifters, whatever that means."

The Girl bristled, as if readying for a fight. The Empress barked to remind her of her place, and who she was here to protect.

"She wouldn't say that to Amma's face."

The Boy laughed, "No. She wouldn't."

After each rock had been marred with the Girl's rune, she waited. And waited.

The ground began to rumble. The Boy gasped. The Empress was familiar with the passing of construction equipment and her current unease was similar.

Mist steamed from the ground like fog boiling away in the sun, but it didn't leave, instead, it clung to the stones, shrouding the makeshift boat. The stones heaved from the ground dragging a phantom keel and boat's frame with it. The ghostly boat rolled toward the waves as if being pushed over logs, sliding into the water without a sound.

The raft of fog trailed the boat, obscuring them from the Viking Village. The Empress smelled the boat's magic and it was familiar to her. It was of a piece with the protections in her harbour. Familiar, but different, a pup to the magic her protections had birthed. Interesting. Having a court magician who answers to *her* instead of the independent contractors the Empress's court typically used could not be overstated. She could thwart Agnes entirely. The couch could belong to the Empress, and the Empress alone.

"What did you do?" the Boy screamed.

The Empress barked. It displeased her when the Boy was upset. Many of his "adventures" with the Girl started this way, not as dramatically as today's, but typically, he'd be filled with worry, then excitement, then remorse. He always forgave the Girl. The Empress knew this, but she wasn't sure *she* would forgive the Girl for taking her onto the water.

The Girl laughed, exhilarated, in response.

"What did you do?" the Boy repeated louder.

"What did I do? What did *you* do?" Another trilling laugh. "This was supposed to be an illusion—like a movie, only realer.

You must've *really* wanted an adventure."

"Don't you put this on me! You *always* do that. You always blame me for something *you* do."

"We're having an adventure. Like *you* wanted."

"The Empress isn't supposed to be in the water. My mom will *kill* me. We don't even have life jackets!"

"She's not in the water, she's *on* the water!"

"Ha, ha."

"Don't worry. We don't drown today."

"Today?" The Boy's voice was practically a shriek, and the Empress whined to hear it. "Wait. What? *When* do we drown? How are you so sure?"

The Empress knew the Girl had an uncanny ability to both get the Boy into, and out of, trouble, but she'd always managed to keep the worst of their mischief from their families. Splashing water slapped him in the face as the prow cut the water, spattering the Empress with misted lake water.

"Get us home! Use your magic! Get us home!"

"Too late now." The Girl shrugged. "We're having an adventure. Be careful what you wish for!"

The Empress had heard those words. About herself. Whenever her court was displeased they had adopted a ruler, not a serf. They cut differently, here.

GIMLI FADED INTO the background. The harbour's clamour disappeared, as did its smells. Only waves and gulls, and the children's delighted laughter remained, their joy almost burying the Thing's stink. Still, the Empress was uneasy. As the shore receded, so did her charge's safety. She was *concerned* for herself. She'd never been this far from land, and the protection it offered. She'd never been into *its* domain.

With the shore's passing from her view, so too did the wards the Empress's charges had commissioned. She wasn't certain who'd made them, but she could sense their protective nature. From this side of the veil, the wards were an insurmountable wall, the jagged etchings abutting each other, linked, and more powerful together than the individual symbols had seemed from the shore. She'd never seen the like anywhere else her court had taken her. In hindsight, the work reeked of the Girl, and yet, different. Also stronger.

"Having fun, your Highness?" the Girl asked, chancing a scratch behind the Empress's ears.

The Empress barked disagreeably in response. She didn't lash out, instead, focused on balancing on the shifting deck. A deck both there and not, like trying to bite a rainbow. You could close your jaws on it, yet you tasted nothing.

The Girl had defeated her. Tricked her. Endangered the Boy, endangered her court, for this . . . adventure. She hated to admit this. They were in the domain of the Thing in the Lake. They had passed the Empress's protective wards, and the Empress's domain entirely. There was nothing she could do now to keep these fool children alive, let alone herself.

Nothing, but trust to luck.

The Boy's terror had faded, transitioning to exhilaration. The one thing keeping the Empress from biting the Girl, to show her dominance. Well, the second thing, she also didn't want to get tossed overboard in the melee, and the Girl was a scrapper.

This adventure was all her fault. She never should've let the boy on the boat. She should've dragged him away—with her teeth in his arm if necessary, and accepted her court's sanction. No, she should've bitten *the Girl*. This was her fault. But she couldn't. If she attacked now, her charge could drown. *She* could drown. And without the Empress's protection, the Thing would surely destroy their home. However, when they were home, the Girl would get *such a biting*.

The boat seemed aimed at the opposite shore, which was only a smudge to her eyes. Was the girl offering them as tribute to the Thing in the Lake? She had clearly seen the beast back on the beach, and still they were here, in its domain. Was the Girl about to serve the Empress to her true master? Well, they'd find the Empress was no easy meal.

She sniffed the air, water, and fish, and plants, and distantly, the campfires from both sides of the lake. Underneath it all, the Thing in the Lake's chemical reek. There was no telling where the beast could be hiding, the lake was vast, no ocean, but deep enough to drown. Deep enough to be lost forever. Anything could hide in its waters.

Something did.

THE EASTERN SHORE grew closer. Trees and beaches came into

focus, and the cabins scattered among them. People on the beaches splashed and played with no fear. The Girl pulled out a stone. Even through the Girl's hand the Empress could feel its shape. The rune that got them into this trouble in the first place. She'd said before she wasn't supposed to have it. The Empress knew, she could sense the Girl's pride and hesitance the same way she herself felt when she stole food from the forbidden platters. A wind rustled the Girl's hair. Her eyes flickered from the shore to the water.

"Okay, let's head home," the Girl said.

The Boy asked, "Sure you don't want to go all the way across and back? Isn't this an adventure?"

She looked at the stone. "I'll be late for supper."

The boat turned for home. They were already too late. As the ghost boat skipped over the waves and troughs as smoothly as a car on a new road, she was certain. The Empress smelled it before she saw it. The wrongness not even one of the largest lakes on Earth could hide.

It was coming.

The Thing in the Lake.

The Empress wished she could warn them properly. She barked and barked, pacing awkwardly from bow to stern.

"Settle down, Marshmallow," the Boy said, with a sigh. "We're going home."

The Girl had also sensed the Thing. The boat, swift as the wind, skipped over the waves faster. The Thing in the Lake followed them. They were defenceless. Helpless. The Empress was too far from her protections. The boat too far from land. They wouldn't have made it to the eastern shore, let alone home. Nowhere to run. Nowhere to hide.

It was here.

The Thing erupted from the water before them, and their magical boat, which had slid neatly over the lake's waves and troughs, pitched precipitously, rocking in the leviathan's wake.

The Empress slid to the boat's bow and only the Boy grabbing her collar kept her from tumbling into the water. He clutched her like a stuffed bear as the serpent rose from the water. A thing of nightmare. A thing that could devour anything it chose. A living world's end. The Empress snarled and barked, howling her defiance. The Thing wouldn't have them without a fight.

"Jormungandr," the Girl whispered.

So. The Thing had a name. And the Girl knew the name. Knew the Thing. There was something in her voice, defiance, not servitude, or deference. An implacable belief that they would survive this day. Foolish, but what else could someone hope to do against such a vast enemy.

Jormungandr's coiled immensity stretched to the horizon, and beyond, as if there were no place the water touched the world the serpent couldn't reach. The beast smelled of fish and rain, but it also smelled *wrong*. Like chemicals. Poison. The Thing in the Lake smelled like death.

The Boy wet himself but the acrid scent of his urine barely cut through Jormungandr's stink. It was hard to tell from the sea spray and splashing, but the Empress would never mistake the fear coming off her charge. Here, in this ocean of a lake, it was all she could do not to tuck her tail and shake. To dive into the water and risk the slow, wet death of drowning. Instead, she growled. She wouldn't allow the Boy to die. Nor the Girl. Not while she lived.

"You are foolish to come out so far, young ones." Jormungandr's voice was wet and vast as all the water in the world. Its conical, curved teeth were each the Empress's size, and there were many. A green trickle misted from its nostrils. A long slender tongue slid from its maw to taste the air. To taste *them*. "I should kill you for your audacity."

"You won't." The Girl Who Almost Belonged sounded braver than the Empress had expected. Recklessness, she was used to from the Girl, but this unseen iron belonged to one who would rule. Assuming, of course, she survived the day.

"You presume much, Skuld."

The Girl stared at the serpent, fists on her hips, the stone clenched in her fist. *She had a hidden name too.* The Empress had never heard the name uttered, yet she knew it belonged. "I survive meeting you."

"*You* do?" Jormungandr eyed the Empress and her charge. "Perhaps *you* do, little Norn, but this is not that meeting. *I* can see things too. Your *friend* is curiously absent from that future meeting. Your fate here—today—is not what you think it is. Your mother cannot save you. Your grandmother cannot save you. Your future cannot save you. The past cannot save you. *Nothing* will save you. Not. From. Me."

"Get us home!" the Boy wailed. "Use your magic! Get us home!"

"My magic is keeping the boat afloat. That's all I can do right now!"

In the distance the serpentine coils rose behind Jormungandr. The children watched in amazement and fear, but the Empress smelled the serpent's feint. So did the Girl. Her eyes flickered, her hair floated, despite the still air. She moved before the serpent. The boat skipped aside, slipping from wave crest to crest, without touching the trough. They bolted for home. The strike came from behind the boat. Beneath the water, from the other side of the lake. Or the other side of the world; it was impossible to say where.

The Girl changed their course. The Empress still smelled dirt, and bird shit, and *pine*. An island. She barked in that direction. The summer had been dry, and hot, and an island, typically submerged, had risen in the centre of the lake, why the Girl thought she'd be safer there, the Empress couldn't say. She didn't know if the town's protection extended there, but it wasn't water. The Thing in the Lake kept pace with them. How could it not. It was *everywhere*.

The island was tantalizingly close. Dangling in front of her like meat on the counter. Every crested wave brought it closer, brought hope closer, and at the same time, Jormungandr's scales tightened. Jormungandr's tail slapped the water and the lake flooded the vessel, washing the Girl's dirt-scrawled symbols from the rocks. The stones fell away from the boat and into the lake when the water touched them. The thin security of the ghostly boat grew thinner. It seemed half the lake sloshed into the boat, scouring the last of the dirt scratched runes. The boat's rocks fell apart and tumbled into the water.

"No, no, no!"

"Naudhiz!"

The children's words blended together into one mantra, even to the Empress's ears.

The rune stone slipped from the Girl's hand. She screamed, "No!"

"You die today, child of fortune." Jormungandr's wet voice gurgled a laugh.

The Empress snapped her jaws over air first, then caught the Girl as they both stretched for the rune stone. The Girl's blood coated the Empress's teeth, she saw the stone plop into the water. Its etched symbol glowed with the same blue as Gimli's wards. Her blood drifted in the water towards the stone. The Empress dove, following its trail. The electricity connecting the blood to the stone was strong. The Girl couldn't be trusted with this power. She snatched the stone in her jaws.

The need stone, the Girl had called it. She wished for land. For safety. She *needed* land. A tide, a current, something unseen, grasped her, swirling around the Empress, the Boy, and, as an afterthought, the Girl. Water gathered them up, and hurled them bodily upon the island.

The island was mostly a lump of dirt and rock. Wave-tossed driftwood created a tangle at the shoreline. A dead tree, large, the island's most prominent feature, and a live one, smaller, were loosely anchored at the island's convex peak. The island bristled with grasses and bull rushes, tall enough to hide the Empress, but not the children. Not from Jormungandr. The serpent's maw hovered over the beach, not held at bay by any wards, this time, merely teasing them. A forked tongue slithered between dagger teeth.

"Give me the stone!" the Girl screamed. "Quickly!"

The Empress kept the stone in her mouth and growled, holding the rune under her tongue. The Girl could no longer be trusted with it.

"Does your mother see you *now*, Norn?" Jormungandr's voice came from all directions, as if the serpent circled them endlessly. "Will her mother weep when she cuts your thread? Do you cry for the future you saw, but will never live?"

The Girl wasn't a fit guardian. The magic had come at the Empress's call. She might look ridiculous, sopping, ridiculous and small, but she'd not let the Thing touch this land. Her teeth were as sharp as ever. She might save them yet. No need was stronger than hers, to protect her court. *Die, Thing*.

The Thing didn't die.

Jormungandr's coils tightened over the small island. Scaled mountains looming to crush them and scour the island to bare rock. Break stone to sand, and let the debris trickle to the lake's floor with their bones.

The Girl pelted Jormungandr with rocks from the beach. Screaming at it to leave them alone. The Empress had to admire her moxie.

"You egg," Jormungandr called. "You unformed thing. You will never live the future you see. If you don't survive me today, you can't live to face me in the future."

The Thing's head reared back and its sickly chemical stink grew stronger. The Empress barked, awkwardly, with the rune stone under her tongue, and focused her will. *Go! Leave us!*

Jormungandr only laughed.

The Girl held aloft a stick with forked branches, and shaped it to have three prongs after the straight end, all the same length. "Algiz!"

She held the stick like a protective talisman as Jormungandr spat its venom. The Empress recognized its power, even if hastily and roughly formed. A gust of wind, blowing against the clouds, dispersed the mist. The rune's after-image remained in the air.

The Girl wasn't strong enough to last forever, and the Empress couldn't make the stone's magic follow her commands. Their landfall had been a fluke. None of her other requests had been fulfilled since landfall. She still felt the tether of the stone's magic to the wards, and their connection to the Girl. The Empress smelled her sweat. Tasted her fear. As could Jormungandr. Misty venom seeped through the serpent's clenched teeth, as it chuckled. He knew they couldn't stop him but the Empress knew who could.

The Girl was an apprentice. Through the stone's tether to her wards, the Empress called for the master, the warding's architect. *Help*!

A shimmer, like sunlight through a window, and an old woman stepped onto the island, interposing herself between the children and Jormungandr. No, not old, ancient. All hard angles and broken slate. The woman smelled of a different time. Of *all* time. A she-wolf among sheep, a goddess among children. Even the Thing in the Lake quailed when her bare foot touched the sand. Its snake head retreated toward the water, its coils loosened around the island.

"Urd." The Serpent's naming of the woman was a dismayed whine.

A look of respect passed between Urd and the Empress, before the stony glare turned to Jormungandr.

"Leave. Do not test me, Son of Loki. I've seen your end once. Your second life is at my whim. Not your father's. Remember this. Remember your place."

Venom snorted past Jormungandr's nostrils. "Another time then."

Urd didn't respond. She didn't need to.

The Girl wouldn't meet her master's eyes, scuffing sand and cupping a stone with her toes. Guilt wafted from her. The Boy had collapsed, clutching his knees to his chest and sobbing. "I'm sorry. I'm sorry."

The Empress moved to the Boy's side. Her presence, her weight, didn't bring him from his despair but it would in time. It always did. She'd protected him from everything else. He would see soon enough.

"I'm sorry, Amma," the Girl said.

"Not yet, but you will be." The woman's voice was steel scraping over stone. Her scent betrayed no emotion. Not fear. Not anger. Not disappointment. She just was. For a moment, the Empress thought none of them would leave the island after all, that they'd traded one monster for another, when the slate visage cracked, ever so slightly. "What has passed is past. We will undo the damage you've wrought, child. We must."

Urd pulled a golden thread from somewhere, drawing it between her fingers. She wound it in a circle around the Boy. The thread smelled of warm toast spread with cheese.

"I will take this memory from him, but he will have no magic in his life. There will be no joy, only heartbreak. Bonds of family will break. His life will be toil. Drudgery. But it will not touch the Nine Worlds. He will be safe from *that*."

The Girl wept. "I don't want this for him."

"*You* made this for him. When you foolishly exposed him to the Nine."

"I didn't foresee this."

"You should have."

The Empress didn't care for the way they were talking about her ward. Not one bit. The Girl wept, her tears mingling with the Boy's as she held him, but he didn't acknowledge her.

"My rune stone," Urd said, holding out her hand.

The Girl's eyes flashed when her grandmother called the need-rune "hers" but she said nothing.

Marshmallow spat the rune into Tilda's hand, watching Urd warily. The Girl cared for the Boy, perhaps she could find a way to save him from her grandmother's "protection." The Empress looked at the Girl. No one could face the stare of the Empress for long, and not do her will, a different source of strength than Urd, but no less potent.

The Girl sighed and whispered the need-rune, *her* rune, and its edge sawed through Boy's golden thread, creating a smaller circle. She tied it around his forehead. The golden light flickered and disappeared.

The Girl whispered to the Boy, "When I'm free of her, you'll be free from this." She paused, gathering the courage to stare down her grandmother before adding, "I can see that much. He's paid enough."

An arched eyebrow from Urd. "Has he?"

THE WITCH VANISHED the way she'd come, gone in a shimmering rainbow, leaving them on the island with a little rowboat filled with the stones from the field in Gimli. "And put those damn rocks back where they belong," she'd called across the waves, her voice, and displeasure, lingering long after the rescue. The Boy was still dejected. He didn't know about the inevitable working of fate placed around his neck. *Couldn't* know. Couldn't understand, and still, he felt it, somehow, because the Empress felt it, and knew his life had changed.

The Girl rowed until her hands bled. Proper penance. The Boy needed her care and companionship. The Empress's tangled fur smelled of the lake. It would take forever to rid herself of the reek, and it would require the shame of another bathing. Her low growl was a groan of resignation.

THEY ARRIVED AT Gimli's harbour, where Agnes Who Didn't Care for Dogs waited. The Empress nuzzled the Girl and chuffed a happy growl, glad to be back on land. Her land.

"You let her go in the lake!"

The woman's anger washed over the Empress. It would pass. The shame of needing a bath would pass. What mattered was she had been victorious. She had faced the Thing in the Lake in battle and lived. She had brought the Boy home from his adventure, even if he was changed, cursed, or both, he *lived*. She'd won against her greatest foe. The Empress stared at Agnes Who Did Not Care for Dogs. The woman's words were nothing. *She* was a monster easily vanquished.

And the Empress shit on the beach.

Davy Bones and the Domestication of the Dutchman

Jennifer Lee Rossman

Having spent my whole life on a ship, sailing the flooded oceans of a post-human world, I've seen a lot of strange things. Desert islands made of mountaintops, civilizations built on massive garbage patches, even a colony of purebred poodles intent on keeping the prizewinning pedigree alive in a world without dog shows.

But this . . . *this* is new.

"It's floating, right?" I ask my first mate.

Bonnie growls softly, her ears back. "It's floating," she confirms.

"And kind of . . . is it glowing, too?"

"Yup." She marches toward the cannons as fast as her tiny legs can move.

"Where are you going?"

"It's weird. Gonna shoot it."

Groaning, I cast an uneasy look at the luminous ship hovering just above the last rays of sunset on the horizon, and go after her. Though she's a mutt like most dogs these days (excluding the poodles), Bonnie's got a lot of Chihuahua in her family, and if her size doesn't clue you into that, her attitude definitely will.

"We aren't going to shoot it," I say, nudging her away from the cannons with my paw. I might have used a little more force than necessary, and she skids across the deck, yapping in annoyance. "Just because it's weird, doesn't mean it's bad."

"Yeah, but that's what you said about the squirrel—"

I narrow my one good eye at her. "We don't talk about the squirrel. And anyway," I say, putting my paws up on the railing and gazing out at the mystery ship and its captain mirroring my stance, "it's a dog ship like ours."

That's the closest thing we have to a law on the open seas: dogs take care of dogs. Doesn't matter if we know them, doesn't matter if we like them. We protect each other, we trust each other.

I howl our standard greeting, but the other ship doesn't respond. Just floats there until we lose sight of it in the morning fog.

"REMIND ME WHY I trusted the otters?" I bark as we give chase, paws on the wheel and ears flapping in the wind. The last slice of sunlight frames the other ship, silhouetting its skinny shape and tall masts.

"I believe the phrase 'They're basically just water dogs' was mentioned," my old sheepdog navigator, Rufus, drawls.

"And there was treasure involved," Bonnie points out, "and treasure is awesome. Unlike otters." She jumps up on a crate next to me and barks her little head off. "No good, two-timing moist weasels!"

Well, never again. Yes, the otters can dive down to the ancient civilizations and bring up valuable artifacts from the human era, mementos of our dearly departed partners in evolution, but they can also run off with the artifacts. There are some who are trustworthy, but I'm getting too old and my muzzle is getting too grey for this to be worth the trouble.

A projectile whizzes past me, buries itself in the wood of our foremast. I growl. "Bonnie—"

"Violence?" she asks hopefully.

I wish she wouldn't phrase it like that, but I wag my tail in the affirmative. "Try not to sink it, just ruin their day a little. I want our treasure back!"

"No fun!" she says, running for the cannons.

She gets off one shot before Rahjai starts howling the alarm from the crow's nest. "Incoming ship," the hound calls, "starboard!"

It's our weird, floating friend, glowing bright against the encroaching dark of night. But she's close; how did she get so close without anyone seeing?

I stare at the ship, forgetting the otters for a moment. Something isn't right. It looks like a normal ship, has all the right parts, but the proportions are just a little off and not everything is in the right place. Like someone copied a ship without really understanding the purpose of what they were building.

Without warning, the mystery ship veers sharply in the direction of the otters. Too sharply; it shouldn't be possible. But it draws their fire away from us, and the way the otters are scrambling around on the deck gives me the impression they're panicking, feeling outgunned.

"Bonnie, cease fire! Rahj, give those moist weasels an ultimatum!"

"Crew of the *Amazonian*!" he bays, his deep voice carrying like thunder. "This is your only warning! Return our treasure or sink with it!"

Moments later, the crates are pushed overboard, splashing into the ocean one by one and bobbing on the surface where we can retrieve them. The otters speed off into the night, leaving us with the mysterious ship, which appears to have sustained no damage even though I can't fathom how the *Amazonian* possibly could have missed it.

The captain is standing alone on her deck, close enough for me to get a proper look. She seems wild, more wolf than dog, and simply massive. My ancestors were Newfoundlands and German shepherds; I am not small by any stretch of the word, but the wolf captain is at least as tall as me, if not slightly taller.

And she glows in the dark just like her ship.

Bewildered as I may be, I am still a gentleman who remembers his manners. I lower my head in a gesture of gratitude; she does not wag her tail, but I see the wagging in her eyes just before she and her ship vanish, taking one of our crates with her.

SHE'S A GHOST.

I've never met a human, but dogs lived with them from the very beginning until the very end when everything got hot and the oceans swallowed up their world. Their culture became our mythology; that's why my cabin is decorated with some of the more interesting treasure we've found over the years. I might not personally know the significance of pearls on a string or a little plastic lady in a grass skirt, but they help me feel a connection to my ancestral best friends.

It's this reverence for humans, this gratitude for making us who we are, that gets passed down through every new generation of pups, faded by time but still lingering. Like the ghosts they believed in.

My crew stares at me with varying degrees of skepticism as I explain the concept. I guess maybe my family was more interested in human culture than theirs were, if they don't know about ghosts.

"So humans believed that when something dies," Rahj says slowly, "sometimes it comes back, but it's not actually back? It's just . . . air and bad memories?"

"So it's like a fart," Bonnie says.

"No—"

"*Yes*," she argues. "When I eat food, it dies in my tummy and becomes a ghost fart."

I blink at her slowly to acknowledge her comment, and steer the conversation back to its original route. "Humans believed ghosts happen when someone dies without being truly satisfied with life. They come back to try to fix it so they can rest peacefully."

"Then where are all the human ghosts?" my quartermaster challenges. "They destroyed their world; I'm supposed to believe they died satisfied?"

She has a point. Maybe the human ghosts are down in the deep with the rest of their civilization. Maybe that's why we sink our dead, so we can keep them company like our kind always has.

I am about to bring up that possibility when Rufus tilts his head to the side and asks, "But . . . what do we do about ghosts?"

"Oh, I know!" Bonnie growls, ears back and tail wagging in anticipation. "We bust 'em!"

"No, Bonnie," I quickly shoot down that idea.

"*Yes*, Davy. There's a whole song about it. My grandma taught me. I thought it was about goats, but this makes more sense."

"Somehow, I doubt that." I heave a big sigh. "I guess we try to help her with whatever is stopping her from finding peace."

THE GHOST CAPTAIN comes back every night without fail, just as the sun's warmth leaves and the chill of night starts creeping in. Sometimes circling us, as if patrolling for danger, but more often than not just sitting companionably at our side.

She doesn't seem to have a crew, just a big, empty ship, but she still carries herself like a captain so that's how I think of her. She's friendly enough, greeting me with a small nod every evening. Hasn't spoken or otherwise reciprocated my attempts at communication, but I like the routine. Makes the nights less lonely.

The sound of tiny nails on wood alert me to Bonnie's presence before she joins me on deck, exchanging nods with the wolf captain before falling into our comfortable silence. Of course, this is Bonnie we're talking about, so the silence doesn't last for long.

"So, any luck with the fart wolf?"

I cover my face with my paws and tuck my tail between my legs. "*Bonnie.*"

"What? She thought it was funny."

Looking up, I see the wolf captain *is* indeed smiling, her mouth open and her tongue lolling slightly.

"See?" Bonnie snuggles up close, burying herself under my fluffy fur.

"Comfy?" I laugh.

"Mmph," is her contented response as she uses my company to ward off the chill of the night.

Just like our ancestors did with the first humans. Venturing out of the forests, drawn by the warmth of the fires and the promise of trading scraps of meat for protection against the humans' enemies.

That was the start of everything. Of them gaining the symbiotic upper hand to become as amazing as they were, of us being domesticated and finding our purpose as man's best friend—

Oh.

I look up at the ghost ship, at the feral captain who shows up just as the cold creeps in, keeping us company and protecting us. It's only now that I notice the longing in the captain's eyes, like we have something she has been denied.

"You aren't a wolf," I say to her. "I've met wolves, and you're not like them. Not the kind we came from, anyway. Not the kind the humans loved."

She crosses her paws in front of her, lays her chin on them sadly. There's something under her paws, a bundle of fabric mangled and torn by time and ocean currents.

A doll. Part of the treasure she helped us reclaim from the otters, most likely. Maybe she misses humans, too, or misses what she could have had. Why else would she pick the doll, a miniature representation of the masters and companions she could have loved?

"You never got your chance, and now you're gone and they're gone and you feel like you'll never get a chance to be domesticated and have that relationship."

The wolf captain sighs, and I echo the sentiment. I have no idea how to help her.

I'VE NEVER REALLY had a purpose. Never thought I needed one. I have my ship, I have my crew, we travel the world and have adventures and sometimes there's treasure. What more could a pirate dog need?

But I want to help the ghost captain find what I have. Family, community. Because it isn't just *my* ship keeping me warm and protected when the sun goes down; *every* dog ship looks out for one another, howls a greeting whether we know each other or not, whether we are mixed breed mongrels or purebred poodles. It's part of our shared cultural heritage, passed down from those first good boys and girls who shared their lives with humans.

I want her to have that, to know that love I've never felt personally but which still runs through my veins. I want her to have it so much I'm afraid it's becoming my purpose, and I'm afraid I will end up all floaty and glowy when I die because I can't help her.

"There's no humans left," I say to the ghost captain when she appears, our ships so close that they would be touching if hers was solid.

She nods, staring at her paws and lowering her tail like she should have known better than to hope.

"We've looked everywhere," I apologize. "Asked everyone. If there were people left, even ghost people, someone would know about it." I even asked the otters, on the slim chance that a colony had survived in some sort of underwater dome. Nothing.

The captain doesn't make a sound, just stands there pretending to be stoic, but I can tell she's trying very hard not to whine.

I can't imagine her devastation. If she is as prehistoric as I think, she must have been trying for thousands of years to find the human companionship extinction deprived her of. Probably inspired a lot of legends of big ghostly dogs around the world.

And then the floods came and people died out, so she made herself a ship because that's what dogs do now, and she sailed around the world until she found someone who wanted to help.

But it still doesn't matter, and I hate that.

Somewhere in the distance, there's a howl as one ship greets another. The response comes a second later, higher pitched than the first. Usually that's the end of the exchange, but we must be near a port because another voice joins in, and another, until the night is full of singing dogs letting each other know that we may be strangers, but we aren't alone and we never will be.

From various parts of the ship, I hear my crew adding their voices, and I might not feel like contributing to something so joyful right now, but I can't resist, either. My howl rumbles through my body, deep and instinctual and ancient.

And then there's another voice, so beautifully primal that I stop to listen.

It's the ghost captain, her luminescent head tipped back to the heavens as she sings with the desperation of someone finally finding something they didn't even know they were searching for. I join back in, and we sing late into the night.

I don't know if she'll be back tomorrow evening, but if she is, she knows she'll be welcome to ward off the cold and loneliness with us.

JOHNSON THE TERROR

MEGHAN BEAUDRY

SATURDAY. THE CITY animal shelter. I'm not here by choice. My classmates in the Winston College creative writing program drift among the cages, cooing and pointing out the cutest dog, the fluffiest cat. I push the brake button on my wheelchair and wait near the front desk. The aisles are too narrow for me to fit—an excuse to avoid venturing deeper into this labyrinth of unwashed fur. I pull my notebook from my backpack. In a moment, bodies will fill the folding chairs arranged in the waiting area. Community members, but mostly students' parents, will listen politely as we read, then hopefully leave with an animal—part of Professor Gould's initiative to bring literature to the underserved. Because the only thing less appealing than the scent of dog poop wafting through the air is undergrads reading stilted lines about losing their virginity or their parents' divorce.

Most of the seats are full by now and I manoeuvre my chair towards the front—I'm the third in line to read—when I feel something wet on my elbow. I turn to see a slobbery tongue retreat back into a cage. An animal that's more mop than dog peeks at me through shaggy bangs. He can't be more than fifteen pounds soaking wet, which, judging by the smell of him, was not too long ago. He holds his left front leg in front of him as if it's hurt.

A woman in an SPCA shirt misinterprets my stare. She unlocks the cage, scoops up the mess of matted fur, then deposits him in my lap. She flashes me that unabashed animal-lover smile—the kind that assumes you're okay with dander and dog breath just because she is.

I squint at his hurt leg and then look up. SPCA lady answers my unspoken question, and not in that slow, over-enunciated way people use when they're trying to decipher whether my wheelchair use translates to an inability to understand human speech.

"His paw was amputated before we rescued him. He's been adopted a few times, but they keep bringing him back."

The canine disguised as a dirty janitorial tool licks the armrest of my wheelchair. I push his hair out of his face. Brown eyes stare up at me, a touch of milky cataracts over one pupil.

I don't want to be a punchline. The disabled guy with the disabled dog. The man whose legs don't work and the dog who's missing one. But Shelter Lady's words bounce around the inside of my skull like a child's rubber ball: "they keep bringing him back." I read my piece along with the rest of my classmates. Then before I can stop myself, I slide a handful of crumpled bills over the counter for the adoption fee. "Thank you, sir," SPCA lady says. Then she smiles like she knew all along.

I HOOK THE dog up to the leash I'd bought at the shelter and wait fifteen minutes for the city bus, huddled under the bus stop in the freezing drizzle. The dog wriggles under my jacket. He shakes, splattering droplets over my glasses. The sky looks like God ran out of blue. The bus's brakes scream as it stops, sending a tidal wave of water over the curb. I reach for my joystick before I realize it's the bus with the broken wheelchair lift. Twenty minutes later and I can't tell who's shivering more, me or the dog. A second bus pulls up. The driver lowers the lift, then scowls at the rangy mutt in my lap.

"He's an emotional support animal," I lie. The driver eyes my wheelchair and says nothing.

I live off campus, which costs about four hundred dollars more per month. I wasn't late registering for classes, but apparently I was late enough that the few handicapped rooms on campus were already booked. Once inside my apartment, the dog sniffs. I lower him down onto the floor. He hops around the perimeter. Cautiously, as if he's deciding whether my cramped studio is up to his standards. I watch him for a moment, then turn on my computer. I pull up my novel in progress—a young adult murder mystery about a teenager with cerebral palsy who wants to be a detective. Lately, writing has felt like a long slough up a muddy ramp. Frustration had formed a ball of tension in my chest, then sunk down into my gut where it has festered for the past few months. I'd started with a clear outline, but I'd begun to question everything—mainly, would anyone even want to read this? I move a few sentences around, delete some adverbs, and then the words dry up, unlike the weather. I open my browser window. The familiar chatroom pops up on the screen. A black pirate flag with a skull unfurls across the top.

Wheels207, Crip1987, and SkipToTheLou are deep in the middle of a discussion. I've only ever met Sam (Crip 1987)—one summer at Camp Capable when I was fourteen and he was thirteen. He has spina bifida like me.

Try being fat. Get on an airplane and watch the looks you get. Crip1987's avatar is a cartoon of a pirate with an eye patch waving a cutlass.

A cartoon Bluebeard pops up. Wheels207. *Joke's on them. The worst thing about sitting next to me on a plane isn't my weight. It's my motion sickness.*

I take a picture of the dog with my phone, upload, and post. *Newest member of the pirate clan.*

Sam, Lou, Wheels, and I have been chatting for years. We haven't always called ourselves pirates. Two years ago Lou shared a meme of a pirate with a peg leg and a hook for a hand.

No leg? No problem. No hand? Put a hook on it. No eye? Here's a patch. Deaf? Man the cannons, your glorious bastard! Pirates are not here for your ableist crap.

Within the hour, we'd all changed our avatars to pirates.

Doggo's picture loads. The appropriate oohs and ahhs appear on the screen.

What's his name? Wheels asks. Suggestions pop up on the screen. One sticks out to me: a little-known pirate from the 1600s named Johnson the Terror. He sustained seventeen wounds in battle and survived, only to be hanged as soon as he recovered—

a tidbit of history our Pirate Crew found maddening.

That's society for you, Lou typed. *Disposing of what it doesn't find useful.*

Technically they don't have to. The world will kill you slowly all on its own, I type. I think of Lou's insurance company last year, denying his prescriptions. I think of the four short steps leading up to the entrance of my university, and the wheelchair ramp so steep I have to rev my chair to get up.

After I log off, I take Johnson the Terror outside for a walk. He sniffs the grass, then licks the concrete like it's ice cream. After ten minutes of him not peeing, I lead him back inside. Immediately, Johnson lifts his leg on the corner of the couch, dousing it in urine.

"You *are* a terror," I tell him. He looks me in the eye and wags his tail.

I TAKE JOHNSON the Terror with me to my writing workshop the next day. I'd tucked my notebook in my backpack, then stopped to survey the scene before rolling out the door. The piles of computer cords and stack of textbooks looked less like college life detritus and more like a delightful array of chew toys. Johnson lay curled in a circle on the carpet, his nose touching his tail. He's cute—the picture of innocence—but I remembered the couch from last night. "You're not fooling anyone," I said aloud, then reached for the leash.

Someone has spilled a frappuccino in the middle of the wheelchair ramp leading to the liberal arts building. The overturned plastic cup sits in the middle of the ramp like a traffic cone, pink and white liquid staining the concrete. I try to manoeuvre around it. No dice, and I've left my Grip-It at home. Johnson looks up at me from my lap and yawns. "Way to earn your keep," I tell him. I back up, skirt the perimeter of the parking lot, and enter the building from the ramp in the back.

I'm late. "He's a seeing eye dog I'm training," I lie to Professor Gould, although I get the impression he wouldn't care if I showed up with a miniature pony. "His name is Johnson the Terror," I add.

"He doesn't look like a terror," coos a senior with pin-straight blonde hair. Aside from commenting on my work in class, she's never spoken directly to me before. "What's wrong with his leg?"

she gasps. Johnson manages to affect a look of tortured deprivation. He nudges her hand until she pats his head.

"He's missing a paw." Over the course of Johnson's life, I'll find myself explaining this to strangers so often I'll consider having a T-shirt printed. It'll go in my dresser right next to the one Lou sent me a few birthdays ago—*Are you ignoring me because I'm Asian or in a wheelchair?*—emblazoned across the front.

"You're such a good person for adopting him even though there's something wrong with him," my classmate gushes. I guess she doesn't see my expression, because that look of giddy self-assuredness never leaves her face.

Class starts. We critique the essay a student in a Hawaiian shirt wrote about his service trip to Africa. Then we read someone's poem about Autumn that uses the word "crisp" no less than fifteen times. When it's my turn, we discuss my latest chapter—the one in which my main character foils a fellow student's plan to rig the student council election. Johnson seems content to sit on my lap. Whether this is born of a need for connection or sheer laziness is anyone's guess.

"I love how sparse your language is. Hemingway-esque," the blonde girl says.

"Excellent use of active verbs," someone adds.

Hawaiian Shirt glances down at his notes on my manuscript. "But would he be strong enough to carry the ballot box up the stairs like that? I mean, physically?"

"That's what I was wondering, too," a student in the back says. "But I like how he doesn't beat us over the head with his disability. I mean, we don't have to hear about it every page, so it doesn't get boring."

"Although I think the character is so brave for going to school even with a disability," the blonde girl adds. "*So* brave."

"I hear it's required by law," I say, even though the writer whose work is being discussed isn't supposed to speak.

"What's the cure for what the character has? When he gets better, does he become a detective?" calls out a student in the back.

"It's a brave story. Very brave. But you *do* want your able-bodied readers to be able to relate," Professor Gould says. It's a line I've heard before—from both the agents I'd submitted my work to.

I can feel myself fading into the background as the voices of my classmates swirl around me. My wheelchair disappearing, my skin morphing from tan to grey to match the cinderblock wall behind me. I think of the freezing drizzle outside the bus stop yesterday. How the first icy pellets shocked me, but how once my shirt was damp enough, I stopped feeling each individual raindrop. How over time, it's not even about the zap of cold droplets. The grey sky, the cold damp air all melds together to create this depressing, inhospitable environment. There are times when being surrounded by able-bodied people feels like a dreary winter day. My body itself is never the problem, but people will never stop assuming that it is.

That feeling of being overlooked, ignored, misunderstood permeates the world like cold, damp air. And no one gets through life without breathing.

THE CITY BUS smells like burnt rubber and cabbage on the way home from class. The driver raises an eyebrow as I roll onto the wheelchair lift with Johnson the Terror in my lap. "How's the emotional support animal?" he asks.

"Great. I'm feeling less . . . emotional," I say.

He says nothing. When my stop comes up he glances at me, but I don't pull the string. Johnson pokes my hand with his nose until I pat his head.

I get off at the next stop—the city park. Johnson wanders beside me on his leash as I head towards an area sectioned off with a chain link fence. *Small Dog Park—Under 20lbs*, the sign reads. Once inside, I unhook Johnson's leash. He lifts his leg on a patch of grass, then hops off to explore.

A dachshund waddles towards its owner, a short man in a brown coat. I'm reminded of that saying, the one about owners and dogs starting to look alike after a while. The only way the man could resemble his dog more was if he wore a hot dog suit. I glance at Johnson and make a mental note to get a haircut. A Pomeranian and two Yorkies race around a metal water fountain. A German shepherd and a husky wrestle over a tennis ball, their owner oblivious to the size limit.

"Your dog hurt his leg," an older woman on a bench nearby points. The sun glints on the crochet hooks in her hand. A yellow and blue blanket spills from the hooks onto her lap. Her legs swing under her, too short to touch the ground.

"He's missing a paw," I tell her. Twenty yards away, Johnson the Terror sniffs a corgi's butt.

Concern flashes across her face. "I'll crochet him one," she promises.

"He gets around just fine," I tell her. "There's nothing wrong with him."

Just then, I look up to see Johnson trot towards the husky. The larger dog's teeth are bared as he hovers over the tennis ball, growling at the German shepherd. I push the joystick and jolt towards him.

The husky lunges at the German shepherd. In the flurry of paws and teeth, neither of them gets the tennis ball. Then from the fray emerges Johnson the Terror, ears flapping as he darts away unscathed. He's practically levitating, bounding across the field with the kind of speed no one would expect from a three-legged dog. His mouth is open in what looks like a grin, the yellow tennis ball clenched between his teeth. A true pirate in every sense of the word. The bigger dogs never saw him coming.

He's halfway across the field before the husky and the German shepherd know what hit them. One flying leap later and Johnson is on my lap. His toenails leave scratches on my arms. Dirty paw prints mar my white shirt. Inexplicably, I remember the query letter for my novel and the list of literary agents on my computer. I haven't touched them in months. I feel a spark of something bright–like a glimpse of the sun on a dreary day. A true pirate doesn't wait for permission; he goes after what he wants. I reach for the slobbery tennis ball in Johnson's mouth, but he refuses to let go. Like any pirate worth his salt, he's tenacious to the end.

Ghost Pirate Dognapper

Kristen Brand

I WAS WORKING in my home office when I heard Bea stomp down the stairs, her car keys jingling.

"Are you going grocery shopping?" I called, thinking of our empty fridge. "Can you add flaxseed to the list?"

"What the hell's a flaxseed?" she shouted back. "And no. I'm meeting a client."

I jumped out of my chair and raced to the kitchen just as she grabbed her wallet off the counter. Bea's a tall, intimidating-looking woman, her muscular arms covered in sleeve tattoos. Dark-haired and brown-skinned, she wore torn jeans, an old Metallica T-shirt, and a pair of cowboy boots.

"What client?" I asked. "You didn't say you had a new case. Can I come?"

I let Bea room with me rent-free, and in exchange she let me tag along on her paranormal consultant jobs when it worked with my schedule. It gave me great opportunities to practice witchcraft.

Bea glanced away. "Uh, I don't know if anything's going to come out of this one. Honestly, if she didn't live in town, I wouldn't bother going to meet her. But things have been slow lately, so I figured why not."

"What's the job?" I asked.

Bea looked back at me and sighed. "She says a ghost pirate stole her dog."

I stared at her for several seconds, barely blinking. "Oh my gosh, please let me come. Give me thirty seconds to grab my purse. I'll be right back."

A short drive later, we met Ms. Judith Dorsey at a little café in St. Augustine Beach. I figured she was the client based on her "Dog Mom" T-shirt and tearful, red-rimmed eyes. She was petite and blond like me, though her hair wasn't nearly as curly as mine and was streaked with grey.

"Ms. Dorsey." Bea walked up and offered her hand. "I'm Bea Romo Reyes. We spoke on the phone. This is my associate, Maggie."

Instead of shaking Bea's hand, Ms. Dorsey clasped it pleadingly with both of hers. "Please tell me you can help."

"I can't make any promises, ma'am, but I'll do my best."

We ordered drinks, Ms. Dorsey getting a latte when she looked more in need of a soothing cup of chamomile. Then we took seats at a secluded table in the corner, and Bea got straight to business.

"Why don't you walk me through what happened?"

Ms. Dorsey pulled out her phone and showed us a photo of a fluffy little Yorkshire terrier wearing a red bow. "This is Jane Pawsten. I've had her for about five years now. I always keep an eye on her when she goes out to do her business because I live right on the water. Last night, I let her out as usual. I stepped away for a second when my phone rang, and when I came back—"

She made a choked sound, and her hand covered her mouth. "I never should have taken my eyes off her. It's all my fault."

"It's not your fault," Bea said gently. "What happened when you came back?"

"I saw him." Her voice went low, nearly a whisper. "He was faint. Like a cloud almost. He wore a three-cornered hat and tattered old coat, and his beard was a tangled mess. He looked at me, and I knew—I knew he took Jane. Then he just faded away."

She broke off, sniffling, and I glanced at Bea to see what she thought. Her forehead was creased, arms crossed as she studied Ms. Dorsey. Had the woman really seen a ghost? Or had something more mundane (but equally tragic) happened to Jane Pawsten?

"I'll take a look around tonight," Bea said finally. "Let's talk rates."

So after sunset, we found ourselves in Ms. Dorsey's backyard. She lived right on the river, water lapping rhythmically against the shore. Lights from houses on the opposite bank reflected off the dark water, clouds hiding most of the stars overhead. The air smelled brackish and carried a hint of something rotten. Algae maybe, or dead fish.

Ms. Dorsey's lawn was neatly trimmed. She had a small dock that extended a couple dozen feet into the water, though it was weathered and lacking a boat.

Bea pulled out her pendulum, a neat little crystal on the end of a silver chain that pointed her toward the nearest source of supernatural energy. She held it out and waited, but it didn't move so much as a centimetre.

"No ghost?" I asked.

She stuffed the pendulum back in her pocket. "Not now, anyway."

"So what do you think happened?"

"The dog probably drowned or got eaten by an alligator or something." She ran a hand through her messy hair. "I'm really not looking forward to breaking the news to the lady."

"You don't know that for sure," I argued. "Maybe—Maybe it got dognapped."

"By a ghost pirate?"

"By somebody dressed as a pirate. We should ask around at that pirate museum downtown."

"Uh-huh. Because that's really the most likely explanation."

"It's possible." I crossed my arms. "We've seen weirder."

Bea snorted but didn't argue.

"Or we could wait?" I suggested. "See if the ghost comes back again tonight?"

"Probably not worth it." Bea kicked at a piece of bark lying on the grass. "Some ghosts appear in the same place almost every night, but most . . . They might show up once a year, if that. People lose track of time when they're dead."

So if a ghost had stolen Jane Pawsten, what did that mean for the poor little dog? Where was she now?

Bea huffed. "I guess we can try a summoning."

"Great! I think I have a candle somewhere . . ."

I dug around in my purse and found a thick white candle. Bea and I sat on the grass (after checking it for dog poop), and I held out the candle to her.

"Seriously?" She glowered. "You didn't bring a lighter?"

I shrugged unapologetically. Who needed a lighter with her as a friend?

Grumbling, she reached toward the candle. A flame sprang to life on her fingertip, and she touched it to the wick.

"Thanks." I set the candle carefully on the ground between us, then I closed my eyes and took a slow, deep breath, focusing on my intent. When working magic, it was best to keep things as simple as possible.

"Spirit who took Jane Pawsten, come forth."

The flame flickered in a breeze but didn't die, and a shiver went down my spine despite the hot, humid air. Frogs croaked somewhere along the riverside, and the rumbling of passing cars came from a distance. I surveyed the dark yard and placid waters, searching for a blurry figure or ghostly glow. I didn't see anything, but these things take time.

We waited.

And waited.

"Right." Bea stood about half an hour later and brushed grass off the back of her shorts. "This is a bust. Ms. Dorsey was probably seeing things."

I blew out the candle and got to my feet, disappointment weighing me down. "What are we going to do?"

"Make up some psychic bullshit about sensing that Jane Pawsten is in a better place and then refund half her money out of guilt," she answered, trudging back toward the house.

Dragging my feet, I followed. Poor Ms. Dorsey. Poor Jane Pawsten. I wished we could do more.

A cold breeze brushed me from behind—unnaturally chilly for a summer night. The wind moaned somewhere off over the water . . . Or was that really the wind? My skin prickled, and I looked over my shoulder.

I stopped walking. "Bea."

"Hm?" She turned and followed my gaze. "Well, damn."

Drifting down the river in a haze of fog was a skeletal old ship. Its black sails were shredded to almost nothingness, and its broken, beaten hull didn't look particularly watertight, except . . .

Was it sailing through the water or hovering over it? I couldn't say. Movement on the deck was barely visible, figures swimming in and out of sight like a mirage. The whole thing looked as if it had voyaged out of a nightmare.

And echoing across the water from the eerie phantom ship was a faint, high-pitched barking.

BEA AND I came back the next night with a boat. It wasn't much, just a cheap little motorboat that we'd borrowed from a friend of my grandma's who took it out fishing. It made a puttering noise as Bea drove us to the centre of the river around where we'd seen the ghostly pirate ship the night before. Then she cut the engine.

The air seemed unnaturally quiet, our little boat rocking softly up and down. There were fewer clouds in the sky tonight, a waning crescent moon visible amid twinkling stars. I could see a bridge in the distance, houses and other buildings lit up along the shore. But there were no other boats out. We were alone on the water.

"Let's get this over with," Bea said.

I set a new candle on the floor of the motorboat where it would be shielded from the wind. Bea lit it, and I repeated the same spell as before. Then we waited.

Again, nearly half an hour passed before the ship appeared. The fog rolled in first. Seeing it from the riverbank hadn't been so bad, but when it surrounded us, I felt my heartbeat spike with fear. I couldn't see the shore any longer—I couldn't see more than three feet away from us. The moist air made water droplets form on the surface of the boat and dampened my clothes and skin. A shudder went through me, the air more frigid than it had any right to be during summer in Florida.

The dark shape of the ship emerged from the fog. It smelled like low tide: rotting wood and dead sea creatures decomposing in salty air. Its dark, discoloured hull loomed before us. One moment it looked solid enough to touch; then it appeared about as substantial as smoke. Cannons stuck out of small holes along its side. Other gaping, jagged holes looked like the ship had been struck by cannon fire itself—or perhaps smashed against a rock.

The old vessel creaked and groaned, shouts and footsteps audible from the deck above. Then Jane Pawsten started yipping.

No one seemed to have noticed us yet—assuming any of the

spirits aboard were aware enough *to* notice the living. I glanced at Bea. What should we do?

She cupped her hands around her mouth. "Hey, assholes!" she shouted. "Ahoy!"

"Ahoy?" I mouthed at her.

She shrugged.

The pirate ship itself seemed to grow still, and a figure became visible on the edge of the deck. A dark, unkempt beard hid half of his cadaverous face. He wore a long, tattered coat that fluttered in the wind, a sword and pistol hanging off the thick belt that encircled his waist. He seemed washed out and faint, like we were looking through a camera that hadn't quite captured him.

He leered down at us. "Well, what do we have here? Two little ladies lost at sea. Why don't you climb aboard? We could find a use for you."

Chuckles echoed down. I could see the rest of the crew moving about, but they were even wispier than the pirate who'd spoken. None of them had faces, making me wonder if they were truly ghosts or just echoes like the ship itself.

"No thanks!" Bea shouted back. "We're just here for the dog."

The pirate's face darkened. "The dog?"

"Light brown Yorkshire terrier. About this big." Bea held out her hands a foot apart. "Answers to the name Jane Pawsten."

As if she'd heard her name, Jane poked her fluffy little head through the railing on the edge of the ship and looked down at us.

"That's the one," Bea said. "Hand her over."

"Never!" The pirate scooped up Jane and cradled her close to his chest. "This dog is all that keeps me sane while trapped at sea! I'd sooner hand over all the gold and jewels I've plundered than give her up!"

"Her real owner feels the same way," Bea shot back. "She's not yours. You stole her."

"Aye." He scratched the dog behind the ears. "I'm a pirate. Stealing's what I do."

Bea rubbed her face. "Okay, I walked right into that one," she muttered. Then she raised her voice. "You can't take care of a dog! You're dead!"

"No." The pirate's voice rumbled like thunder. "You are."

One of the cannons tilted down with a metallic screech. I

jerked back, rocking the boat.

"Fire!" the pirate shouted.

The boom was deafening. The whole city must have heard it. I shrieked and covered my head with my hands like that would protect me from a cannonball.

I heard a massive splash, and cold water soaked me. The cannon had missed.

The pirate laughed. Sputtering, I looked up at him. Would he fire again? The ghostly ship might look insubstantial, but those cannonballs seemed all too solid.

"That's it."

Dripping wet, Bea surged to her feet. The boat pitched, making her wobble, but she didn't fall. She clenched her fists, fire springing to life around both hands. Heat chased away the otherworldly cold, bright orange flames blazing in the dark night.

"I'm sending you straight to hell!" she shouted, raising her hands to blast him with fire.

I knew this Bea. I'd seen her exorcise demons and fight zombies, battle evil witches and slay horrifying creatures.

But none of them had ever abducted a small, fluffy dog.

"Don't!" I cried. "What about Jane Pawsten?"

I wasn't psychic, but I could see the future all too clearly. Bea's flames would consume the spectral ship. The thing would go up like a leaf in a campfire, banishing every spirit onboard. And Jane Pawsten . . . Bea controlled the fire; she could keep it away from the dog, but what would happen when the ship disappeared? Jane would plunge fifteen feet into the river.

"She can swim," Bea snapped.

"Can she, though?"

Dogs were supposed to be able to swim. Humanity had bred them to be hunters and guardians. But cute little Jane Pawsten with her perfectly groomed fur, trimmed nails, and bright red bow . . . She didn't look like she could handle a particularly deep bubble bath.

Bea's hands fell to her sides, flames dying. "Crap."

What now? We'd found the dog but couldn't get her back. Maybe we could climb onto the ship and take her by force, but I didn't see a ladder and doubted the ghost pirate would throw one down for us. He seemed more likely to shoot us in the face with a spectral bullet.

What would we tell Ms. Dorsey? *Jane Pawsten's started a new life on a ghost ship. Sorry we couldn't get her back, but her new undead owner really seems to love her.* That seemed almost as bad as telling her the dog had drowned.

"Right." Bea plopped back down into her seat. "Your turn."

"My turn?!"

"Yeah, I played bad cop. It's good cop time. See if you can reason with him."

I looked up at the ghost pirate and swallowed. He glared down at us, his eyes black like oil pits. The way he kept stroking Jane Pawsten reminded me of a James Bond villain.

"But how?" I asked. "He loves that dog."

"Yeah . . ." Bea peered at him. "Maybe we can use that." She straightened from her slouch, suddenly full of energy. "How would you say that ship sank?"

I looked at its broken hull, its sails in tatters. "I'd guess a storm. A hurricane, maybe."

"Same here." She stood up and shouted at the pirate. "Okay! I get it! The dog's your most precious treasure, and you're not giving her up."

"You're not as dumb as you look," the pirate replied. "If you realize that, then leave. We've no further business."

"But I'm worried," Bea replied. "Is the dog really safe on your ship?"

He snarled, revealing several missing teeth. "There's no finer ship on the sea!"

"But what about the storm?"

His hand stroking the dog went still, and the scowl fell from his face. He stared ahead at nothing, his whole posture tense. He looked haunted—no pun intended.

"The storm . . ." he murmured.

"You remember it, don't you?" Bea prompted.

He must have, because the mere mention of it caused the wind to wail and the ghost ship to rock and bob. The water around us grew rough, and I clutched the edges of our motorboat. Thunder echoed in the distance, and the spectral crew shouted and raced around the deck.

"It's not enough, Captain!" one of the crewmembers cried. "We're going under!"

The ship tilted dangerously. The pirate gripped the railing for balance with one hand, Jane Pawsten held tightly in the other. The dog barked frantically, and a massive wave sprayed the deck. The ghost pirate looked around with wide eyes.

The ship, the faceless crewmembers—they were all constructs of his memories. And now that he recalled the storm, it triggered a replay of the event. He must have drowned during it. I felt awful for him—even if he was a dognapper.

"Give us the dog!" Bea shouted. "We'll get her to safety!"

The ghost ship pitched again, and several crewmembers fell off the edge with screams. There was no splash as they plunged into the water.

"Quick!" Bea yelled. "Throw her down!"

She extended her hands to catch Jane Pawsten.

The pirate stared down at her and then looked at the panicked dog in his grasp. His face screwed up like the decision physically hurt to make. Then, with obvious reluctance, he tossed Jane Pawsten to Bea.

Several things happened at once. Bea lunged forward to catch the dog and lost her balance. The wind howled as both she and Jane fell into the river. Thunder crashed, and the ghost ship lurched sideways, finally overwhelmed by the spectral storm. It disappeared beneath the water.

The fog dispersed, and the wind fell silent. Stock still and soaking wet on the motorboat, I stared around the dark, empty river.

"Bea?" I shouted. "Bea!"

She burst out of the water, coughing and choking, and raised a drenched Jane Pawsten. The dog looked even smaller with her fur all wet.

"Got her," Bea gasped.

Then a frightened Jane Pawsten bit her hand.

Ms. Dorsey burst into tears when she saw Jane. We waited through several minutes of cuddling and doggy kisses before the woman noticed us dripping river water onto her carpet. She immediately offered us towels and first aid for Bea's hand. Bea got the second half of her payment, and we left, Ms. Dorsey thanking us profusely as she hugged her dog.

We climbed into the car and sat there for a few seconds. The towels had helped a bit, but our clothes and hair were still wet.

We both stank, and I could feel dirt and slime on my skin. I desperately needed a shower.

"No more dog cases," Bea said firmly.

"Sure," I replied.

She said that now, but as soon as the next crying pet owner called, her resolve would melt. Tall, tattooed, tough-looking Bea was a softie at heart.

"Stop smiling," she grumbled as she started the engine.

I tried. Really, I did. But I couldn't stop the whole drive home.

Blackbark's Collar

Richard Lau

Ahoy, matey!

Don't encounter many strangers at this end of the wharf, especially in a tin-roof tavern such as this! But if ye be looking to wet your ears as well as your gut, a tale can be had for the small token of a rum and a bit o' silver.

Why, thank ye kindly, good sir! While the good barkeep be fetching our drinks, I shall start a startlin' tale guaranteed to shiver ye timbers.

I was not always the bent and aged critter you see before you now. I come from good, hearty stock. My father kept watch over a flock of sheep in the Fetchtel Mountains in Bavaria before he moved to Ireland. There, he met my mother, who was working as a domestic and arranging tea settings for wealthy patrons. Could the offspring of a German Shepard and an Irish Setter be anything but restless?

So, even though I come from a line of strict landlabradors, the sea called to my fur and heart. As soon as I could get my paws down to the docks, I was off, crewin' fishing trawlers and cargo lines. Never saw my folks again, and call me a scurvy dog, but I never wanted to. Funny how nautical ties are stronger than familial ones.

Eventually, I ended up in the colonial port of Saint Bernard, and after having a wee bit too much to drink one fine evening, I awoke to find the Jolly Rover flying high o'er me head. I had been sharpei'd! Drugged, nabbed, and indentured to serve on a ship or walk the plank!

To make matters worse, I soon realized that the captain o' the vessel was none other than Blackbark, terrier of the Seven Seas! A sea dog so tough, he literally chewed rocks and possessed a foul temperament to match his achin' jaw!

He commanded a fearless and loyal crew of half-breeds: charming and lovable as pugs when filled with rum, but in battle, as vicious and devious as rats. Why, together they were known as the Pugrats of the Caribbean and proud of it, too!

Remember what I said about nautical ties being stronger than familial ones? Soon, I found myself willingly bonded to them by blood, adventure, and glory. I prefixed many of the words in my vocabulary with a hearty "arrrrrrrffffff." I even led chants of "Yowl, howl, yowl, howl, a pugrat's life for me!" Blackbark's ship, *The Pupillon*, was my new home.

Blackbark turned out to be a just captain, leading us to many victories and splitting the booty among us fairly. Except once. We had captured a ship of aristocrats, and the captain lifted a ruby-encrusted collar with a gold medallion right off the neck of an old sheepdog.

"Listen, you curs," Captain Blackbark announced to pugrats and captives alike, "this collar be all mine now. And anyone who dares touch it loses his paws!"

Several days later, as I was bringing Blackbark his supper, I saw the captain quickly tuck the collar under the mattress of his cot.

Was it Captain Blackbark's sudden movement, denying me a longer glimpse of his treasure? Or the intimacy of the cabin, whose wooden walls seemed to close in like a kennel cage on two dogs and a single collar? Regardless of the cause, I heard the mermaid's call as the cursed collar sank its teeth into my very soul. I had to have it.

Despite his hard reputation, the captain had always been fair with me, and I had a bit o' coin saved up. While the collar was beautiful and certainly held a great deal of value, it wasn't worth incurring Blackbark's wrath and his stated punishment.

And so, I went along with my usual routines and ship duties, with the collar always lurking in the back of my mind, like some tightly balled octopus in some dark corner of a coral reef.

Weeks later, while on shore leave at one of the ports that tolerated our thievin' kind and our stolen gold, our captain heard talk about an approaching ship owned by a wealthy merchant from Denmark. This Great Dane was resettling to the port of St. Hubert, and *The Niederlaufhund* would be laden with his treasure and fortune.

We intercepted *The Niederlaufhund* in open water, but they knew who we were, though we had yet to raise the Jolly Rover, and they were prepared, firing their 24-pound canines as soon as we were within range. Blood washed the decks like ocean spray at red tide. Smoke wafted through the holes in our sails, and the crack of splitting wood and splintered timber mixed with the popping snaps of breaking bones.

We were at a disadvantage. While we had to carefully incapacitate *The Niederlaufhund* to board and pillage her holds, the Dane's crew was under no such obligation. The quicker they sent us and *The Pupillon* to the depths of Doggy Jones' treat locker, the better.

But while we were outgunned, we definitely had strength in numbers and ferocity. With cutlasses and pistols tucked in our belts, knives flashing between our teeth, we grabbed ropes and swung over and boarded the enemy ship. In a dog-eat-dog battle, the merchant crew was no match for the Pugrats of the Caribbean!

However, before anyone could reach the Great Dane, he pulled a small wooden carving out of his pocket and, with his anchor-block face twisted in rage, he yelled, "I call upon Poodlesidon, God of the Sea and patron of my family line. Smite these besotted, flea-packin' pugrats! Unleash the . . . Kollie!"

And having made his pronouncement, the Dane tossed the carving into the sea. The statue quickly sank into the deep, dark waters, as if it was made of lead.

For a moment, both crews stopped fighting and watched overboard with trepidation. Large ripples began to form, streams of bubbles churned into pure white foam, and a dog's head, larger than both ships combined and taller than their main masts, rose with majestic and terrifying slowness from the ocean, rivers pouring out from between the yellowed teeth of its gaping mouth. Wagging its black tongue skyward, the creature emitted a thunderous howl at an unseen moon. The Kollie's thick, wet fur resembled a coat of kelp and seaweed. A more arrful sight could not have been beheld before or since!

A forepaw shot out of the sea and came crashing down on the poop deck of *The Niederlaufhund*. A moment later, the clawing was repeated, this time on *The Pupillon*. It was clear that this evil monstrosity cared nothing for and would spare neither ship. The Kollie's long snout swooped down like a sea gull and plucked up the Great Dane, gulping him down like a pelican does a fish, as if to vanquish any doubt of its insidious intent. The dog crews joined together, enjoined against a common enemy, fighting for the very survival of one and all.

I knew we were doomed. Both ships were taking on water and sinking fast. But above the gunfire, screams, and Kollie howls, I heard Blackbark's collar calling to me from his cabin. In battle, one doesn't have time to think, only react. And so, I did.

With the two ships scraping side by side, I quickly jumped back onboard *The Pupillon*, entered the captain's quarters, and freed the collar from its prison under the blankets. When I returned to the deck, I heard a cry of anger coming from above.

Blackbark was hanging from the mouth of the Kollie. And from that vantage point, he easily saw what I had done.

"Ungrateful traitor!" he shouted down at me. "Remember me curse!"

And then the Kollie tossed back its gargantuan head and swallowed him up, curses and all.

My ears rang with Blackbark's warning that he'd cut the paws off of whomever touched his prized collar. But the captain was gone now, wasn't he? Yet another victim of the terrierfying Kollie. So why should I worry? As the saying goes, "Dead dogs wag no tails."

Still, my knees were shaking from the captain's words, as I got into a rowboat and lowered myself into the sea on the far side of the battling ships. I would leave my fate to the ocean and pray to Poodlesidon to spare me.

And for a reason known only to himself, he did spare me. I was the lone survivor, the only one to witness the Kollie submerge once more to the hellish depths from which it arose.

A supply ship rescued me a few days later, and I pretended to have been a passenger on the Dane's ship. I reported to the authorities that the two ships had sunk each other in battle. I was believed. I made no mention of the Kollie, for why needlessly complicate the story?

Can I show you Blackbark's collar? No, I'm afraid I can't. Why? That, my friend, is another story, and a ghostly one, at that! Which I will gladly tell you for another pint and a second coin.

But, for now, be a sport, and help me lift this glass to these withered, wind-dried lips. These hooks are good replacements for paws for many things but are quite useless in hoisting glass tankards.

Let the Water Drink First

V.F. LeSann

"You ask me of my companions. Hills, sir, and the sundown, and a dog as large as myself that my father bought me. They are better than human beings because they know but do not tell."
— Emily Dickinson, "Letters"

THE REFLECTION OF the roaring fire broke and scattered across the dark waves like burning stars, as though the inferno were chasing the ship over the bay. *My* ship, now.

I would've liked to stand at the quarterdeck and sip the bottle of celebratory wine I'd stolen for the ride, watching the estate burn behind me, turning the sleazy bastard inside to ashes. I wanted to do something stupid and poetic, cheering at each tumbling pillar and crumbling wall, writing a manifesto to tuck into an empty bottle and toss into the waves.

But keeping the reins on a full-sized brigantine with a crew composed of one half-drunk fool wasn't exactly leisurely business. So the half-drunk fool in question poured the last of the bottle in the direction of their gullet, hurled the bottle in the direction of the burning mansion with a shrieked curse, and kept stumbling back and forth over the deck, desperately trying to do the jobs of fifteen men at once.

I just had to make it across the bay. And after that, hire a competent crew under the most suspicious circumstances possible. Then sneak out of the Empire. Easy as pissing the bed.

Struggling with an unruly sail, the wet rope slipped and tore through my hands, ripping the skin from my palms. I looped it around my forearm and dragged back with all my strength, salt water bitter on my bared teeth as the rough water of the harbour played havoc with a hull built for speed and agility.

Tonight started with a good ship. And a good crew started with one good sailor.

And if luck was kind to me, I knew just where he'd be.

IT WASN'T THE seediest watering hole on the port, but it wasn't tidy either. Notorious for not asking questions so long as you had coin, it was just the place Faolan preferred.

Shitholes like this were places that I'd been warned away from, and then learned to fear, but now they were a lifeline. Still, tonight my nerves were on edge, assuming the colour of guilt was painted on my face and that the guards were about to storm in and clap me in irons.

I scanned the mingling sailors and dockworkers hunched over meals, women, and ale, looking for Faolan. When my eyes caught him, I breathed a sigh of relief, heading his way and tightening the bandana that kept my wild curls in order at the nape of my neck.

"Connor!" he said with sincere enthusiasm and squeezed me in a tight hug. "What brings you out of the shadows?"

"I've acquired a brigantine," I said, taking my seat and wrapping my jacket tighter around my chest, burying my skin under layers of linens, belts, and a doublet twice my size. "Just pulled her into port, matter of fact. Looking for a crew and had you in mind for first mate."

"You got into port, without a crew?"

I held up my torn hands for proof. "Took a bit longer than expected." It was an understatement; I'd been hoping to be out of Imperial waters by now, as it turned out Mr. Estate was a capital-S someone, one Baron Bjarnson, and word of the fire and the missing ship had spread fast, docking along with me.

Faolan grinned, passing me a drink. "You're doing better for yourself than last I saw you."

We let the rims of our glasses clink and drained our swill,

falling into conversation like it hadn't been a year since we last spoke.

"What did you name her?"

"*Hell's Fury*," I said with a laugh.

"The ocean had a good drink tonight, then!"

I held my smile and drained the rest of my mug rather than answer him. I'd not taken the steps—hells alive, I'd barely gotten the ship docked myself, let alone had the time to write and burn the ship's fool of a name. Later, I could make the time to appease Faolan's gods; right now, I had to get to safer waters.

"You're with me then?"

Faolan clapped my shoulder. "I wouldn't miss it."

"Think we can set sail before dawn?"

Running his hands through his braided beard, he nodded. "Must be worthwhile profit you've found us. I'll see who I can find."

FAOLAN WAS AS good to his word as I remembered. Dawn was only threatening to edge over the horizon when we set sail, leaving faster than a hurricane off the ocean. The waning darkness veiled our departure as Imperial guards doubled on the docks—holding fresh notices bearing a ship that looked remarkably like ours.

Most of the money I pinched from the Baron had gone to provisions, the rest paying off the dockmaster to misplace our information.

Faolan stood next to me watching the port fade into the grey of the horizon.

"First mate looks good on you," I said, jabbing my elbow into his ribs.

"A decent climb from yeoman, don't you think, Captain?" he said, producing a tricorn hat from his satchel. The rich black felt was not new, but carefully tended, framed about with familiar silver lacing. "When Captain Lennox traded the sea for the shore, he gave this to me. Said to find someone worthy."

I blinked back the sudden saltwater in my eyes, leaning down for him to slap the hat on my head. It fit like it was meant for me.

Smiling, he leaned forward, gripping the gunwale. "You've a plan, right?"

"Something 'twixt a plan and a dream," I admitted, "but we can hire out, run cargo. The islands are gold to a sturdy ship."

He nodded at once, but his smile seemed forced. "I hope you're right. Leaving the Empire's a rich man's wager, never mind with such haste. I could've found us a seasoned navigator or a proper surgeon with more time."

Faolan and I had been shipmates three times over, like the wind kept blowing us together. He was curious about the hasty departure and the far-off destination, but he'd let it lie if I didn't bite, and I couldn't think of a gentle way to say "I'm certain the Empire will hang me for murder if we stay."

Regret crept in at the edges of my heart. Not for giving that bastard Baron a one-way ticket to a smoky grave, but for roping good people into my rough waters. I'd only planned to damn him financially—he liked to buy women, so I'd feigned I could acquire them. It was a clean swindle until I found out what he did to the women he purchased, and that his interests grew the younger they got.

And as surely as I couldn't let that lie, I couldn't stay in the Empire.

"Strike while the iron's hot, right?" I said with a laugh. "Besides, did you see the number of ships in port? If they're docked, they're not out making our coin on the islands."

"They won't be there to take cuts off our profits either." His dark eyes stayed fixed on the water. "It'll be a long trip."

"Ship's built for it. Is the crew?"

Sparing a glance behind me at the crew he'd rounded up, he gave an optimistic smirk. "They look better than we did our first time on the sea."

WHEN I FIRST decided to stake my claim on the sea, it was impossible to get work as a woman. What was the difference between the labour of woman or man, I'd argued with the merchants and dockmasters. Women were bad luck at sea, so Connor had been born out of necessity. He was as much me as I was, but not the lady the sailors feared would sink their ships.

IN THE END, Faolan's optimism wasn't misplaced, the crew was better than we deserved. Most of them were half-starved from a working camp, barely old enough to shave. They learned fast and built strength hoisting the rigging and ropes.

The first night I'd taken dinner in the mess with the crew, I'd seen a crowd of them staring at the chunks of dry bread Cook plopped atop the stew like they were precious enough to weep over. I'd not taken my own stock of the crew, trusting Faolan's eyes as my own: they were all limbs, the lot of them.

"You can have two pieces," I commented, amused. "Build your strength. Ship work is hard business."

The fella nearest me twitched like I'd hauled back to hit him, colour flooding his face.

"Wouldn't dare, sir," he mumbled, pointing his chin to another boy. "They smashed Colburn's hands to pulp for takin' more than his share. I heard him groan three nights afore they sent him away for goin' cripple."

My stomach twisted, my hands flexing on the edges of my bowl.

"He does the ropes fine though, sir. That's what Selwyn was goin' to say," Hadley, another young and too-thin crewman I'd helped learn the wheel, added quickly, giving a sharp elbow to Selwyn, who I now recognized haunted the crow's nest. "Colburn can write with his left now, and does more than his share of the work Faolan gives us."

"Captain's rule," I announced, raising my voice. The mess hushed quicker than I'd expected, eyes rising warily. "No-one's served aboard the *Hell's Fury*. Take what you like. I trust there'll be no hoarding and no gorging, and that we can all work a ladle well enough to give Cook a break."

In the days that followed, nervous glances slowly turned to easy conversation, and full bellies lightened spirits. And when we finally sailed out of Imperial waters I felt like I took my first breath since the fire.

Faolan became a figurehead at the stern, staring at the ocean we left behind. The deck was nearly empty, all but a few of the sailors snoring in their hammocks below, and there he was, a shadowy watchdog gleaming in the silver moonlight, mesmerized by the waves.

"See something out there?" I asked, standing alongside him, hoping the answer was no.

"See? No. Feel, perhaps." He sighed, running a nervous hand over his bicep. "It's nothin'."

"Tell me. You know I'll listen."

He took a deep breath and his worry lines melted, taking age with them. It was easy to forget he was a younger man when he fretted even more than my grandmother had. "I feel like the ocean's angry with us, Connor."

"Angry with us?" I repeated with more levity than I intended. "That's better than you saying you think the Fleet's on our rudder."

He shot me a dark look and touched wood. "Damned wretched thing to suggest."

"And an angry ocean's not? Mine's a reasonable, nautical worry." Faolan and I had developed a friendship by neither asking nor telling. It made it easy to make a friend without getting familiar, which I appreciated. I never asked why he took his meat so raw, and he let my past stay dead where it belonged.

"Careful, you'll get that Captain's paranoia."

"Me? You're the one who's lingering like a ghost at the stern every night." I moved closer to the edge and his arm caught mine, probably gripping tighter than he meant to. He was nervous. "What's got you rattled, Faolan?"

Tugging my arm, he pulled me well back from the gunwale.

"A fool's worry."

"You've never been the fool. What is it?"

Faolan exhaled, running his hands through his dark hair. "The ship feels peculiar."

"How?" I asked incredulously, gesturing up to the mainsail. "This's a prime specimen of a ship."

"No, not like that. I mean, she looks grand." Rolling his eyes, I saw the regret edge into his expression, probably wishing he'd said nothing at all. But I waited, giving him the space to finish.

"The ship . . . the ship smells sour. Like she's rotting. I know how it sounds, Connor, I do."

"It'll be a priority at first light. We'll check the hull. If any of it's rotten we . . ."

"I checked it yesterday," he muttered, "and again this morning. The boards are sound."

Taking a step back, I gave him a smile. "I believe you."

"Well hell, that makes one of us," he said with a wry snort, shaking his head. "It's nonsense."

"We'll look again in the morning, first bell. I trust your instincts." I shrugged and glanced off the starboard bow into the moonlit night. "You were always the first to know when we were near a storm or about to stumble into one, like you could smell it in the air. Made our time at sea a lot more pleasant."

"Too much brine in my blood, I suppose."

"Any way it came about, I'm damned thankful for it." Clasping his shoulder, I gave it a tight squeeze. "We'll check again at first light."

SUPERSTITION DIED WITH my grandmother, but her blood still burned in my veins, because when we hit the doldrums I was certain they were the rot Faolan had smelled, since the hull was in pristine order. Weeks with no whisper of wind, days with long stretches of heat pressing down on a glassy sea, and nights bearing no reprieve. I'd heard stories about sailors dying in the 'drums, or worse, going mad in the endless nothing.

Faolan had never looked worse. His dark skin was not only chapped but seemed to cling tighter to the bone, and he'd stopped blinking altogether. We took shifts for the crew, but lost days between us.

The heat made me disinclined to keep diligent about my dress. Layers of clothes became a strangling noose in the unrelenting heat, tempting me to forgo my farce of hiding all womanly indication under linens twice my size. I fought the urge, fear stronger than the pull of madness. Dare the crew discover me a woman during the doldrums, it'd be unanimous to either throw me overboard or use me to fill the impending void of food.

Luckily, we maintained our sanity, and as our resolve began to wane the wind finally took a long-overdue breath.

But barely did we get the sail up than the wind turned sour and the breeze we'd cheered for shifted into a whipping gale.

Behind us the sky was clear, but the wind pressed us like a juggernaut's fist, forcing us towards clouds that billowed on both the starboard and portside, blazing alight with shocks of green lightning.

"We need to go back!" someone yelled, their voice high and breaking with panic.

"And fight the wind? Are you daft?" Faolan hollered against the howling gale.

"We fight the wind or we go right into the angry eye of those squalls." I strode across the deck, tying the belt on my coat in triple knots as I'd abandoned my doublet in my quarters like a fool.

"Cap'n, off the stern. Unless my sun-bleached eyes deceive me, sir, I see sails!" My heart sank, a heavy anchor to the excitement in Selwyn's voice. He was leaning halfway off the crow's nest, adjusting his spyglass. "Aye, ships, four. Bearing Imperial colours! They've come to save us!"

I swallowed hard, feeling the wind kick our ship like a fallen drunkard at the bar. Barely keeping my footing, I gripped the gunwale and held onto my hat.

"Cap'n, sir? Fleet ships approach from the stern," Selwyn called again.

"How far off?" I yelled, pushing my voice as hard as I could so it wasn't devoured by the gale.

"Barely off the horizon, Cap'n." The exhilaration disappeared from his voice, replaced by the cruel realization they'd never reach us in time if the storm swallowed us. "Another wind," he said, yelling down to me, "pulls their sails east, while this one presses us south. We're divided."

A blessing or a curse, I couldn't decide but I pushed it from my mind, throwing my all into pulling the rope in my hands. "Get those sails down or we lose them! We're not going into that storm without a fight. We'll get no respite from the Fleet today!" If it was between the storm or the Fleet, I'd have taken the Imperials, a better chance to throw my hat to fate and spare the crew. But that choice was gone now. Now we fought the raging skies and the ocean's wrath.

Faolan ran the length of the deck, getting everyone to their feet and barking orders as I thought of them, while I dodged a fury of briny waves crashing on the deck, struggling to reach the wheel. Hadley had the spokes in a death-grip, knuckles white as he leaned into the wind.

There was a crack like thunder just as I made the quarterdeck, but the sound was close and too sharp to have come from the skies. And then came the groan of wood that would turn any sailor's blood to ice.

"Foremast's coming down! Brace yourselves! Cut the ropes if you can reach 'em!" Faolan was on the opposite side of the ship but I could hear his voice louder than anyone's, as if the wind carried it to my ears. My eyes shot up to see the foremast, the top quarter torn asunder, clinging with splinters of wood precarious as toothpicks.

The lines off the foresail thrashed in the wind, still bound to the deck. "Get those ropes off or she'll drag us down with her!" I roared, taking the wheel from Hadley.

Faolan rushed through the veil of rain, two knives in hand slashing at every rope on the foremast. The mast creaked in the wind and shuddered as the slivers gave way, and she plummeted down, caught by a gust of wind and carried into the dark waves.

"Go!" I said to my wheelman, "go secure the sails on the mainmast before we lose them too! I'll keep her true."

Hadley gave me a curt nod, the whites of his eyes glimmering with fear. "Weeks we prayed for a breath of breeze only to get a screaming wind."

"That's why I avoid praying. Scurry."

The wheel tried to tear me down, forcing me to use all my strength to keep her level. The storm was trying to swallow us into the giant's gullet and I wasn't about to be a meal without a fight. I'd clawed to survive my whole life, I wasn't willing to become a ghost easily. The clouds roiled from east to west, clashing like two titans in a barroom brawl. The ocean crashed, waves smashing the side of our ship, shoving *my* brigantine towards the fight.

"This ship's mine, you greedy cad!" I screamed, gripping the wheel with my nails and holding my feet firm. By inches my grasp slipped, my arms growing weary and my boots scrabbling to maintain purchase. I squeezed my eyes closed and hung on with every muscle I had. "You can't have her!"

The wheel lightened by a pound and it was enough for me to open my eyes. Faolan was beside me now, gripping the wheel with long nails imbedded in the wood. "Let her go!" he begged, the cacophony of the water and thunder muffling his words. "We stand a better chance getting through it if we go in. Ride the damned storm."

"I need this!" I yelled back. "The ocean can't have my ship!"

"Nor shall she. But if we spend our wind with the first punch, we'll not last the fight. We're already weak and tired from the 'drums. We need to bide our strength to last the brawl."

Swearing under my breath, I shook my head. "What if there's no getting through? You saw the crosswind that waylaid the Fleet. What if there's no wind at our backs to escape?"

His grip slipped on one of the wheel's spokes, sending me almost off my feet, as he sunk his nails into the next one and held onto the sodden wood with a white-knuckled grip. I hadn't realized how much strength Faolan was spending to hold the wheel steady.

"Then I'd ask you which gods you've pissed off today, Captain," he laughed, groaning as the wheel tried to break from his grasp again. "If we stay this course, we lose her now. This round's not to us, but perhaps the next will be."

Seconds bled into heartbeats as our gaze settled with one another. Finally, I grimaced my acceptance.

"Steady on, lads," I called, "secure your lifelines. We'll give her hell from the inside!" Giving a nod, I bobbed my chin in count and on three we released the wheel. The ship lurched, finally relenting to the heave of the ocean throwing us into the eye of the warring squalls.

We ran to the bow. Faolan outpaced me with each stride, seemingly more steady on the teetering, sodden deck than he'd ever been. Lightning blazed overhead, making everything spark green. Every crewman I passed, I clapped on the shoulder. "Hold fast, lads, the next round's ours. And first round's on me once we hit port!"

Once I caught up with Faolan, we stared into the midnight abyss our ship raced towards. The ocean slammed into itself, as we sailed on the knife's edge where the two storms met. Vicious swells from each side crashed like fists, only the smaller ones were broken by our hull. The larger ones sailed over us and rained briny fury on our heads, snatching any unsecured object—barrels, crates, coils of rope—away with watery claws.

"I've never seen anything like this," Faolan gasped, gripping my arm with his free hand. "It's unnatural."

"Damn me to hell, you were right," I said, feeling the rage welling from the east and west, colliding at the path of our ship, knowing now that anger was meant for me, for *Hell's Fury* that didn't belong on the ocean.

"I'm right about a lot of things," Faolan said, his humour strained with rising fear, "you'll have to specify."

"Does she still smell 'rotten'?"

Faolan furrowed his brow and gave me a sidelong glance. "Yes. Worse now."

"It's because we are. The ship's rotten. I'm rotten." I cursed, scrubbing the water off my face. It poured from the brim of the tricorn that I suddenly felt ill-suited to wear. "I've doomed us all."

"Don't lose your nerve on me now, Captain."

"Devil take you, Faolan, listen to me! I didn't do it right, I pissed off the gods I don't even believe in," I said, begging tears not well in my eyes. "I didn't . . . I didn't change the name. I didn't burn the old name . . . well, I think I burned most of the name by accident in the fire . . . but not the right way. I didn't give the ocean the first drink. I didn't do any of it!"

"Why?" Faolan exclaimed, his eyes wide with confusion and blazing with betrayal.

The raging winds dragged the words out of me like a thief under the poker. "I killed a man and ran. Ran with his ship until I found you, the only crew I knew I could trust. I didn't think the ocean cared, I didn't have time, I didn't . . . the Empire is going to hang me like a dog."

"Not if the ocean eats you first." I could see the muscle of Faolan's jaw twitching and he couldn't look me in the eye.

"He didn't deserve this ship," I pleaded. "He didn't deserve his money. He didn't—"

"His lack of worth isn't cause for you to die along with him," he snarled. "The Ledger of the Deep has the wrong name, and the ocean will eat you, this ship, this crew unless it's set right."

Panic rose in my throat like bile. "If I throw myself to the ocean's mercy, will she stop?"

Faolan winced, hanging tight to my arm and the rail. "No. It's the ship she doesn't know. It's wrong, foul, rotten to her. It's like sickness, a gangrenous limb that needs the surgeon's saw."

"Hell," I whispered, "I've sunk us all."

"Connor, I trust whatever you did was right. I know your heart is good. You're brash, and sometimes a fool, but not bad. Never that."

Glancing back to the crew, the boys were all tied tight to the main mast, eyes either closed tight or bugged in horror; there was little left to do but pray.

Faolan tore off his jacket and pushed it into my hands. The sea rumbled beneath us like an angry mountain. The waves had settled for a breath as we moved into the eye, but the clouds churned and the wind still thrashed like an angry behemoth.

There was just enough of a space of quiet for us to hear the ship groaning as she pitched.

Pressing his jacket back to him, I grabbed his hand as he fussed with the buttons of his shirt. "Might give the boys a jolt to see flesh before death, but let's assume no one is dying today."

"I think my *skin* will be the least of their jolts," he said removing his clothing. His skin glistened in the rain, glowing through the blazes of lightning. Again the ocean rumbled under us as the sea surged, waves growing once more with doubled fury. "Your fate's with the Mystress of the Deep now. A bargain must be struck or she will sink us."

"How the hell do we do that?"

"Meet her. Bargain." He grinned hopelessly. "Something 'twixt a plan and a dream?"

Faolan's flesh twisted with the shadows between lightning strikes, skin giving way to scales and then fur slick like a seal settling over top. His bones creaked and his body contorted. A snout grew from his nose and his fingers webbed like fins, his hands hit the deck with paws to match his feet and his spine stretched into a long scaled tail. Barbs sprung from his back like sharpened daggers, thin skin tight between each spike. Dark eyes met mine and a voice rang in my thoughts with more of a rumble than usual.

Her lair is too deep for a human to dive, but I know the way, Faolan said in my mind. *If you do the steps, she may be willing to bargain. If not, the gods'll call their beasts if the waves can't bring the vessel down. Kraken and leviathan and the rest not fit for stories.*

I took a step forward as in a trance, running my hand over where sharp scale met long spine. "You're not a bit human, are you?" Shaking my head, I pulled my hand back. "We can discuss later."

I'm a sea dog, he rumbled a laugh in his throat. *Listen to me now. Burn the name on paper, offer it to the corners. The ocean must drink first, the best we have. Explain. Do the steps, Connor.*

If Faolan trusted me with his truth, I could trust him with mine. Neither of us was going to die today in unfamiliar skin.

In one swift motion I tore off my hat and bandana, letting my hair fall in unruly curls. I wrenched the wrap from under my shirt, which had always broadened my chest to the masculine, and hurled to the deck.

"I'm Nell O'Connor, not Connor O'Nell." My unfamiliar voice rasped out without Connor's forceful baritone, and I tasted the name that felt like a lifetime ago, that was so unfamiliar I didn't recognize it anymore.

He stretched onto two legs and used a front paw to reach for my hat, grasping it with sickle-like claws and placing it back on my head. *Let's go with Captain, then. It suits you.* He spun his body like a seal and dove off the side, disappearing into the churning depths below.

I took breaths between heartbeats, staring into the wine-dark waves, hoping for some sign he wasn't dead, but the thunder roared like a demon and the lightning lashed like a whip, and the ocean didn't share her secrets.

The steps. He'd told me to take the steps. I turned to the crew who were pale as ghosts. The sea resumed her onslaught on our vessel.

"Colburn?" I called.

Shakily he stepped forward, lifeline still wrapped around his waist, and gave me a tremulous salute.

Clapping him on the shoulder, I tried to rouse him from his stupor. "Haven't you ever seen a sea dog before?"

He looked from the spot Faolan had disappeared and then back to me, shaking his head. "Only read about 'em."

"Well, you're in luck. They're a blessing from the deep. The scoundrels of the Mystress herself." I shook his shoulders until some colour returned to his cheeks.

"Cap . . . ma'am?"

"Captain."

"You're a woman . . ." His voice trailed off like he'd just uttered a curse in a church.

"Astute."

"Women are . . ."

"Bad luck!" came my barrelman's voice from behind him. When I looked back to the bulk of the crew, about half wouldn't meet my eyes, the others staring in betrayed horror. Well then. If I brought them through this with their lives, they could throw me overboard.

"You listen here, lads. The only bad luck you'll find is being a fool. And I was foolish. We'll fix my mistake and hope the goddess takes pity on our ship." I untangled the braided twine from my neck and handed the key to my quarters to Colburn. "I've heard you write, Colburn."

"Yes, Cap'n," he said, taking it with his left hand, and turning it over with nimble fingers. "Poetry and scribbles mostly."

"This key bears the ship's former name. Scour the brass until it no longer reads the *Humble Daughter*. Take Selwyn with you to my quarters, search all the papers and burn anything with the name, or drown it in seawater until the ink's no more. Understand?"

"Captain," Selwyn stuttered from behind Colburn. "If the gods are angry, what hope do we have?"

"Anger is never a reason to hurt, gods or no." I curled Colburn's fingers over the key and gave it a tight squeeze. "The *Hell's Fury* will not sink today."

"The rest of you," I shouted, "will bail water, patch the hull, secure the lifelines. We'll not go gentle into the deep!"

The cheer that followed was scattered at best, but nobody wanted to die. The crew got to work and so did I, digging through the crates tied below the quarterdeck as the ship shook, now truly at the mercy of the ocean. Finally, I prised open a crate packed with bottles and grinned when I saw the French script on the wax seal. This would do. Another boom on the starboard side and the hull groaned—it would soon give way to the onslaught. I just needed the ship to hold together a little longer.

I found some well-kept parchment in the crate, with large, flowing signatures, and pressed my nail into my forefinger until I bled. On the parchment I scrawled over their seals and signatures that assured the authenticity of the alcohol. The *Humble Daughter* rang out in fresh red. I mused over what that meant to a man like Baron Bjarnson who thought girls were better in his bed than safely with their mothers.

I fumbled my tinderbox from my pocket, flint snapping a flurry of sparks onto the mercifully dry paper that I desperately shielded with my body. I held my breath as the parchment darkened, smoked, and finally caught.

The parchment burned, flames devouring the old name. I rushed to the deck, a full bottle tucked under my arm, shielding the burn from the wind until it was time. Once topside I held the paper overhead letting it linger to each of the four winds in turn.

"Hear me now: I'm renaming this ship. Better late than never. The previous owner was nothing but a piece of shit and I stole it, and I will not sail under something named the *Humble Daughter* when the tastes of the previous owner make that name sour. I'm late because I ran . . ." I did my best to explain until the paper was nothing but ash.

With the knife from my boot, I cut the top off the bottle, letting the glass shatter near the neck. More of it broke than I'd planned and half the liquor was already in the ocean. "Looks like you drank a lion's share first. Here's to your thirst. Don't you drown my crew for my foolishness." What was left I held high, saluting the clouds that meant to sink us and let the rest of the wine wash over my face and open mouth.

What I could do was done, but the storm raged on. I clung to the gunwale, barely staying on my feet, staring into the abyss for any sign of Faolan. To the east the waves tremored, and the planks screamed as the quake shook. A column of water shot to the sky like a dragon and detached from the ocean itself before arcing closer to our ship and plummeting back into the deep. The waves hurtled into us, and I lost my footing, sliding across the deck until my lifeline grew taut, slamming me back onto the ship.

The hit shook me to the bones and I stayed flat. Stars burned in my eyes, melding with waves that towered over my ship and the blur of my vision came together to see a figure as large as the sky looming, sneering at me. She was both a wave and a woman, and the most beautiful thing I'd ever seen, with clouds and lightning churning around her like a dress of storms. The torso of a woman with wings billowing behind her like a swimming ray. Tentacles wider than our mast slid onto the deck and twined around the gunwale until the wood screeched in protest.

"You are arrogant." Her voice was the wind and rain, the crash of waves and the nothingness of the deep. It chilled my bones and burned my stomach. I couldn't bear the sound and yearned to hear her again. Forever.

"You're magnificent," I stammered, choking on water that fell in my gaping mouth, which tasted sweeter than ever before. The boards beneath us shivered in time with what my wild thoughts told me could only be the heartbeat of the ocean. It drummed through my ears, my blood, my heart.

Faolan hopped aboard like an errant splash, standing

protectively between me and the Mystress. *Don't say anything, Captain.*

The wave-woman bubbled, the echo of laughter dancing sharply with the crash of lightning.

Mystress, we ask you to accept the renaming of this ship, add it to the Ledger of the Deep, and let us sail your seas. Faolan strode closer to the wave, settling in the shadow, his tail swinging like a metronome, dark eyes trained on the goddess.

"The steps have been taken. But you," she said, letting a smaller tentacle trail my cheek, her eyes burning a blue I now saw swell in Faolan's own. "You now have a debt with me for your transgression, hasty one. I will add your name . . . if you pay."

"If I do this," I said, "you'll spare the ship and crew?"

"Yes," she preened, letting lightning twine in her fingers.

Captain, don't make a bargain I'll live to regret.

"Name your terms, Mystress." I was willing to give her everything, but the crew wasn't on the bargaining table. She could have me, my bones, my servitude for eternity—but not them, not even for a second.

The ocean crackled with her delight. "You have a penchant for spilling the blood of unworthy men. That's a gift I can use. I have a quarrel with a Spaniard you may settle. Find the ship bearing one Padre Buel, and remind the lot aboard they serve the Mystress of the Deep. Have them fear her sea dogs, and our debt is settled."

I hadn't taken my eyes off her, hypnotized by the rhythm of her waves, but I had enough wits left to speak. "Begging your pardon, Mystress, but Faolan's the only sea dog here."

"Oh?" Her voice was high and short, but it was less a question than a sound. "Is he?" Her grin was wicked with a spark of mischief.

The wind twisted back upon itself, unfurling in the opposite direction. I was struck with the sensation of being stock-still on firm ground while the sea raced below.

There are few of us left, m'lady, Faolan said with an apologetic bow. *Most have returned to you to slumber. I've never met another of my kind.*

"You have now. Our deal is struck, Captain?"

I probably would have followed her back to the depths and asked her to marry me right then, but instead I gave her a bow of my own, my hat at my chest. "The deal's good, m'lady. When we're done, they'll remember your name or scream it while they're dying."

The waves at her back preened, manta ray wings fluttering in the glimmers of lightning bursts. "Then sail, my sea dogs."

The wave collapsed, filling the ocean to the brim and our ship spun wildly across the leagues. I grabbed Faolan and pulled him to me, gripping him tight though his scales and spines cut my raw skin, letting my lifeline secure us both to our ship. I could hear the crewmen yell and wail, but thankfully no screams faded into the distance as we finally came to a stop in the bright sunlight, with the wind at our back.

I grinned at Faolan and gave him the tightest hug I could, feeling his scales melt into skin and his bones return to familiar shapes.

The crew got to their feet from their scattered spots, all treading slowly, carefully, unsure of their footing. My eyes met each of theirs in turn, seeing the same blue glow edge their pupils I saw in Faolan, in the goddess. As they saw, I suspected, in my own.

"We're alive, lads!" I exclaimed, and we all laughed, grateful and joyous laughs. The deck was full of fish for us to eat and when I ran my tongue over my lips I could taste the briny water quenching my thirst.

The shadow of the Fleet snuck up on us in our celebration and before I could blink we were boarded. Faolan had managed pants and his tunic, and I tucked my hair under my hat, and did my best to tighten my jacket over my sodden and tattered linen shirt.

The Commodore of the Fleet was dressed in royal colours with enough regalia that it nearly sagged his jacket, and was shadowed by a shorter, grim-faced man bearing a parchment.

"Who is the Captain of this vessel?" he demanded.

Swallowing, I took a step towards him, half expecting my crew to shove me forward and mutiny right there. I'd been an awful captain, and a liar, and wouldn't blame them in the least. After a breath, when no one grabbed my shoulder, I raised my hand at the Commodore.

"I am, Commodore." I put the false baritone back in my voice and kept my face shadowed under the brim of my hat, hoping he wouldn't look too hard. But I knew the purse of my luck had been emptied twice over today.

"Captain . . . ?" His voice trailed off expectantly.

I moved to speak, but Faolan spoke first. "This is Captain Nell, Commodore." His hand was on the back of my hat and he slid it off my head, shaking off the extra water before securing it back on my head after my long hair had spilled free. "She's the Captain of the *Hell's Fury*."

The Commodore stared, and his clerk gasped, hastily rereading their parchment. "A woman?!"

"And we're her sea dogs," Hadley added from somewhere behind me, more confident than I'd ever heard him before.

I glanced back to see them all on their feet, behind me and Faolan. Arms folded, backs tall, and chins proud as though they wouldn't be moved. My heart swelled ready to burst with pride.

"This . . . this can't be right. Gentlemen," he said chuckling, addressing everyone but me, "having a woman aboard is wretched bad luck."

"With all due respect, Commodore," Selwyn said, "I've been told the only bad luck is being a fool."

"I've never heard such a thing," said the Commodore, who had intended to add more but his clerk interjected, whispering fussily in his ear.

My ears sharpened with new precision and I easily overheard them.

"This ship doesn't bear the markings of the *Humble Daughter*. The colours aren't right—this one doesn't bear the right figurehead—some woman with tentacles at the front. That vessel was stolen and captained by a man—we didn't get his name, but the dockmaster was clear about that at least. This ship . . . I don't know who the devil they are, but it can't be our quarry."

With a nod, it was clear the Commodore agreed and wanted off our ship as quickly as possible, like the ill-luck of my sex might be catching. He turned sharply on his heels, sparing a glance to everyone except to me, who he gestured the sign of evil towards. Faolan stifled a laugh.

"Apologies from the Empire for slowing you down, Ca . . . Captain." Gods alive, he could barely say it. "We were mistaken about your ship. Fair winds and following seas." With as much decorum as he could muster, he descended the ladder to his gig. I could hear him snapping out his irritation at his oarsmen as they carried him back across to his ship.

The Fleet was leaving, but I was frozen in place, staring at them as they departed. Air caught in my lungs and I didn't have the words or the stomach to face the crew.

A hand clasped my shoulder. "Captain, the *Hell's Fury* is yours."

I turned to meet Faolan's gaze, taking a deep breath. I wasn't sure how I missed the subtle pulse of the ocean in his eyes before, the mark of the sea dog it seemed, but now it was so apparent I couldn't see anything but the touch of Mystress there. "A bit too much brine in your blood, eh? Who knew it was a catching thing."

Faolan chuckled and ran a hand through his beard. "I've never had a pack. It feels good."

The sentiment felt right, like I was on a ship with family. Like we breathed together. "Strange, though. All of it. Had you ever met her before?"

"The Mystress? No, just heard stories. When the storm comes in, or the waves crash right, sometimes you hear her sing."

"And you can swim down deep to her lair?"

Faolan stifled another laugh. "Thinking of making the trip down? It wasn't that easy, my friend—stretched my lungs to the brink."

"I've had worse ideas, haven't I?"

His hand squeezed my shoulder and his brown eyes gleamed blue. "Don't fall in love with a goddess, Nell. Seems all bad."

"Nothing's all bad." I laughed with him then and we clasped hands. "But really, how'd you think one goes about proposing to a god? The usual flowers and jewels?"

Shaking his head, he squeezed my hands hard, giving them a good shake before letting go. "I could knock some sense into you and you'd still probably try."

My gaze circled the ship to the crew, all above deck, bearing the same blue-eyed gleam I felt howl out of my own.

My eyes fell on the wheel, still and proud, and I walked to the helm.

"Where to, Captain?" Faolan strode as my shadow and it felt truer than anything I'd ever known, the posture was somehow right in my blood.

"Gentlemen, I believe we have a Spaniard to hunt. Let's drop what sails we have left and let the wind bring us to him."

Ten voices cheered, bellowed, howled to the sky, and the wind answered, filling our sails, sending us north.

New Tricks

ALICE DRYDEN

THE GREAT AIRSHIP moved almost silently through the evening sky, its eight powerful motors churning and its canvas envelope tinted gold by the setting sun. Vast. Majestic. Shaped like a bone. Far below, white-tipped waves swished across the turquoise sea like wagging tails.

In the gondola of the *Cavalier King Charles*, cocktails were being served.

"I say. What's an air pirate's favourite aperitif?" The speaker, a pug, beamed up at the stewardess pouring his drink.

"I don't know, sir," the Dalmatian lied.

"A dry mArrrrrtini!" He yapped with laughter and nudged his wife, who rolled her eyes.

"Gin and tonic," she requested, "and better make it a large one."

"Good evening, everyone. This is your captain barking." The passengers fell silent as the soothing tones of the Old English sheepdog came through the speaker system. "We're making good time thanks to a tailwind, and we will be mooring for the night in approximately one hour. Until then, please enjoy your drinks and dinner. Passengers on the port side—that's left—can enjoy the magnificent sunset over the Galapawgos island chain, and the famous Moon Bay, alleged to be inhabited by a savage tribe of wolves untouched by civilisation. Those seated to starboard may be able to see . . . *air pirates!*"

The deep, calm voice broke off in a panicked yelp, and chaos reigned in the gondola.

Passengers on the starboard side scrambled to get away from the portholes, while those seated to port scrambled starboard to get a look. The pug spilled his mArrrrrtini, climbed into his wife's lap, and trembled. The Dalmatian stewardess readied the first aid kit.

A swarm of four swift and deadly biplane aircraft was flying in formation towards the *Cavalier King Charles*, black against the sunset they had used to conceal their approach.

In the cockpit, the captain made a frantic distress call.

"Mayday! Mayday! This is the airship *Cavalier King Charles* calling the Dog Watch! We are under attack! Please hurry!"

In his panic he forgot to close the channel that broadcast to the passengers, and his yelps boomed through the gondola. Realising his error, he added, "There is no cause for alarm. Please stay in your seats. Stay. Stay!"

A new voice spoke over the tannoy, gruff and reassuring.

"Do not worry, *Cavalier King Charles*! The Dog Watch is on the way. This is Agent Buck McLusky barking. ETA three minutes."

Buck McLusky! Buck McLusky the husky! The blue-eyed— well, one blue- and one brown-eyed—hero of the Dog Watch! Despite the peril they were in, a thrill spread through the gondola. Tails began to wag cautiously, and there were a couple of excited whimpers.

But the pirate planes were closing in fast. Now the watching passengers could see that each craft was painted a different colour, so they formed a dancing rainbow in the sky. The leader was white, decorated on the fuselage with a pink flower.

"The Dog Rose!" yapped a beagle puppy with his nose pressed to a porthole. "The most feared and famous air pirate of them all!" He wiggled at the prospect while his parents shuddered at the name and pressed together for comfort.

The captain watched helplessly from the cockpit as the planes buzzed the airship, circling it and darting in and out. "Like fleas," he muttered, scratching his floppy ear. There was no way his giant craft could evade or outrun the pursuers; all he could do was hold his course and hope.

Machine guns stitched a line of dark holes in the bone-shaped envelope, which began to billow and sag. More shots took out five of the airship's eight motors. The pirate craft surrounded the *Cavalier King Charles* on all sides, forcing the captain to descend until the gondola brushed the waves below. The lead plane dived steeply, landing on the water beside the stricken *Cavalier King Charles*, followed by the other three. Foam sprayed up around their floats as they coasted along.

"So beautiful," sighed the beagle pup, struggling as his father tried to peel him away from the porthole. While they wrestled, a grapple fired from the white plane to the airship, pulling the two craft together, and a slim, agile figure leaped from one to the other before entering the gondola.

The Dog Rose was of medium build, but it was impossible to tell what breed she was. Her ears were hidden under her black leather flying-helmet, and two brown eyes glittered behind a matching leather domino mask. A pink silk scarf covered her muzzle. She bowed. The passengers wowed.

"Good evening! I hope you are having a wonderful flight." There was a note of steel in her rich, deep voice. "I won't detain you long—simply hand your valuables to my associates, and we can all be on our ways. But if you try to resist . . ." She tapped the wide muzzle of her blunderbuss. All eyes fixed, fascinated, on the gaping black hole.

"Give her your chew toy," whispered the pug.

"Give her your *wallet!*" his wife whispered back. The Dog Rose passed down the aisle with a bag, in which the passengers placed their treasures: toys, jewelled collars and, in at least one case, a telephone number. A Saint Bernard unclipped the barrel from his neck.

"It's a hundred-year-old cognac," he said sadly, "aged in oak. You should drink it from a tulip glass with just a drop of water to bring out the flavours. Or neat, as a *digestif.*"

"I'll bear that in mind."

When it came to his turn, the beagle pup held out a toy kitten with chewed ears.

"I don't steal from children," the Dog Rose said.

"But he wants to go with you," the puppy insisted.

As he reached up to tuck the toy into her jacket, the door to the cockpit opened. The captain emerged with a spanner gripped in his hairy fist, and crept as stealthily as an Old English sheepdog can towards the Dog Rose.

At the last moment she turned and chopped down on his wrist with her paw. The spanner clattered to the deck.

"I warned you!" The Dog Rose took aim and fired once, twice, three times. Three tennis balls popped from the muzzle of the gun and ricocheted off the wood-panelled walls of the cabin. Passengers and crew alike scrabbled to catch the bouncing missiles, yelping with excitement and scratching the upholstery. None of them noticed the Dog Rose slip away.

A sharp bark recalled the occupants of the airship to their senses.

There were grey hairs on the husky's muzzle, and his ears were nicked from a career of close shaves, but his eyes were bright and clear, and his back was straight as a crankshaft. The passengers neatened their attire and tried to look terribly brave and tough, or in need of comfort, depending on preference.

"Is anyone hurt?" Buck McLusky asked. "Good! Officers of the Dog Watch will be here soon to carry out repairs and see you to safe moorings. Meanwhile, I'll head after those pirates. They won't get away with this."

He ruffled the beagle puppy between the ears and felt in his jacket pocket for an official Dog Watch Cadet badge. "Now, which way did they go?"

Every paw pointed westwards, except that of the beagle puppy, who indicated the opposite direction.

"He's a fan," said his father apologetically.

A frown creased McLusky's forehead, and a shadow passed over his noble eyes. He replaced the badge in his pocket.

"I shall return with your valuables, or else I shall not return at all!" the husky declared. With a graceful running jump, he regained his own aircraft. The propeller spun, and the plane lifted from the surface of the sea, hot on the trail of the air pirates. Husky Buck McLusky vanished into the dusky sky.

MCLUSKY NARROWED HIS eyes, squinting at the golden light that bounced off the waves. In the dazzle, the pirate planes ahead seemed to appear and disappear, the glint from their wings merging with the glare from the sea.

His streamlined monoplane was of the latest design, and he was gaining on the pirate biplanes, but slowly. Westward, the shapes of the Galapawgos Islands broke the flat blue: the larger central isle with its five islets, like the pads of a paw, and the hooked dewclaw a little apart from the main group. Somewhere in there, in the tangle of jungle, was the air pirates' base. No member of the Dog Watch had ever succeeded in sniffing them out once they went to ground.

McLusky growled deep in his throat, the sound merging with the thrum of the engine, and fired a short burst from the nose-mounted machine gun. The rearmost pilot jinked frantically to evade him, losing speed and height before fleeing the battle. McLusky resisted the urge to chase the yellow aircraft and maintained his course.

It was the Dog Rose he wanted.

The other two planes, one green, one bright sky blue, closed in on McLusky from either side, jostling him in an attempt to force him down. McLusky flew straight and level, waiting until they came so close he could make out the whiskers on each pilot's muzzle. Then, opening the throttle wide, he streaked almost vertically upwards. Below him, the other planes collided and spiralled, still locked together, down to the sea.

McLusky's plane jerked, and a line of dark holes appeared in the wing. Distracted by the pirates' fall, he hadn't noticed the white aircraft swooping down on him from above. He pulled the stick back into his stomach and the plane up and over, so it lay on its back as if wanting a scritch. At the top of the loop, with the sea above him and the crimson sky below, he rolled the plane over and dived.

The position was reversed, and now it was McLusky who was above and behind the enemy. He could see the Dog Rose's head turning, checking the sky to see where he'd got to. Suddenly, her plane's wings tilted and it slipped sideways, turning to engage McLusky. The other pilot flew straight for him, despite a volley of warning barks from McLusky's guns, and the husky had to bank left to avoid a head-on collision. A line of holes appeared in the fuselage, and his plane rocked as the other aircraft passed less than a wing's width away.

They circled each other, the two planes almost sniffing each other's tails, neither quite able to get the advantage.

The Dog Rose was good, very good. (As well as *very bad*, McLusky reminded himself.) The husky was constantly jostled and turned during their battle above the waves. The other pilot pushed him lower and lower, nipping at his flank to turn him back east, in the direction he'd come. Bristling, McLusky heeled his aircraft around in a tight bank that pulled his lips back from his teeth. The other plane floated across his sights. Side on, the white aircraft made a juicy target. He wasn't going to fire, though. He would dog the Dog Rose for as long as it took. Sooner or later she would need fuel, and she'd have to head for the air pirates' hideout.

The Dog Rose had no such reservations, and the muzzles of her guns flashed. A pellet struck the instrument panel and ricocheted into McLusky's mouth. He spat it out.

"The fiend! She's firing vitamin pills!" he growled. "And they're not even wrapped in bacon!"

The smells of sea salt and spent fuel were in his nose. Seabirds wheeled below the plane, and he knew the land was close.

His radio crackled, and the voice of the Dog Rose filled his ears, sweet and low. "You'll never catch me, lawdog! You might as well just roll over!"

McLusky growled and leaned forward, willing his plane onward. The edge of the setting sun was touching the sea, a red disc floating in a pink sky. The long shadow of McLusky's plane followed him obediently along the waves, and his tail began to wag.

The voice of the Dog Watch commander barked over the intercom. "Turn back, McLusky! You'll run out of fuel!"

"Negative, Chief. This is our best chance to find out where those rascals bury their bones. Maintaining course."

"You're a fool, McLusky. But a brave one. Over."

"McLusky out."

The Galapawgos dewclaw was approaching fast. The two planes sped towards it and turned tightly, wings almost brushing the pillar of stone. Then the Dog Rose was off among the islands, brushing treetops and skirting cliffs in an attempt to shake her tail. But McLusky stuck doggedly to her.

She obviously knew these islands like the back of her paw, and McLusky dropped back as she shot through narrow gaps and hugged the jungled ground for cover. But the husky's plane was faster and gained a little distance every time they flew in a straight line. Now the two aircraft were almost nose to tail.

The engine of McLusky's plane coughed, missed a beat, stuttered.

"You're running out of fuel, McLusky!" A mocking laugh filled his headphones. "Enjoy cooling your heels on a desert island!"

Snarling, McLusky tore the headphones from his ears. The taunting buzz continued, and he smacked the radio with his gloved fist until it sparked into silence.

The Dog Rose led him back out over the open sea, the wings of the biplane waggling mockingly. McLusky urged his plane onwards, but it was falling behind and dropping lower. Soon he was barely skimming the sea. He pointed the aircraft's nose towards Moon Bay, at the base of the main pad of the Galapawgos, and pulled back on the stick to prolong his glide as much as possible.

The engine gave a last, apologetic bark as the propeller slowed, then stopped turning.

It was a smooth landing that barely made a splash. The plane beached itself on the shore and tipped slowly forward onto its nose as the wheels met the resistance of the sand.

Above him, the white biplane circled triumphantly. McLusky could make out a head peering from the cockpit, and a paw waving in cheeky salute. Teeth bared, the husky drew his pistol and fired upwards.

He intended nothing more than a final show of defiance, but the beat of the engine above him cut to an eeric silence and the other plane began to circle down towards the sea, the air whistling through the wires that braced its wings.

As the white plane struck the sea, McLusky leaped into action. He tore off his jacket and plunged into the waves, dog-paddling out to the wreckage. When he reached the patch of oily water where scraps of wood and canvas floated, he dived.

Twice he dived and twice he popped back up, panting. On his third attempt, he struggled up from the depths with the limp body of the Dog Rose in his arms.

Her dark eyes blinked open. The world's greatest air pirate and the world's greatest paw enforcement officer looked at each other face to face for the very first time. The Dog Rose's lips parted.

"Get off me, bonehead," she said. "I can swim."

CIRCLES OF DAMP droplets appeared on the sand around the two dogs as they shook themselves vigorously. McLusky gathered driftwood and lit the pile with his regulation Dog Watch lighter. Meanwhile, the Dog Rose glared at him. She unwound the soaking scarf from her neck and spread her jacket on the sand to dry. McLusky, stripped to the waist, sat beside her, running his claws through the matted white fur of his chest.

"Maybe you'd be more comfortable if you took that mask off," he suggested.

"Very well. I don't suppose it matters anymore." She pulled off the leather mask, now dark with water and crusted with salt, and shook out her ears. McLusky found himself looking into the face of a rough collie, long tricoloured fur tumbling around her slender muzzle. The firelight flickered in her eyes.

"Nice dogfight. Good moves." She looked him up and down. "Too bad it got you stuck here with me."

"Too bad for *you*. I arrest you in the name of the Dog Watch. You will return the property you stole, show me your hideout, and then it's a long stretch for you. And I don't mean the good kind of stretch, when you're lying in front of the fire with a full tummy and getting sleepy," he clarified.

The Dog Rose's muzzle twitched, and she began to laugh. She threw back her head, flopped over onto her back, and kicked her legs.

"You're funny," she said, looking at him upside-down.

She jumped to her paws, ran over to McLusky's plane, hopped up on the wing and stuck her nose into the cockpit. Her tail, sticking straight up in the air, swished.

"What are you doing?" McLusky called.

"Using your radio to call for help so we can get out of here."

"Ah," said McLusky. "There might be a problem with that."

Her head emerged. "You bonehead," she said. "Now we're really stuck."

"*You're* stuck. A Dog Watch rescue team will pick us up first thing in the morning. Then it's jail for you, Dog Rose." McLusky wagged his tail at the prospect. Bringing in the elusive Dog Rose would be the coup that crowned his long career with triumph.

With this mysterious criminal behind bars at last, McLusky could retire happily to some country estate; spend his golden years terrorising squirrels and marking his territory. "Justice has caught up with you at last. That's what you get for burying bones that don't belong to you."

"My pirates will get here first. Then we'll spit-roast you over an open fire," she countered. "And then I'll bury *your* bones."

"Go ahead and try!" snarled McLusky.

Bristling, stiff-legged, paws raised in fists, the two dogs circled each other. Yellow light gleamed on white fangs as they waited for the right moment to attack. The hush was broken only by the sigh of the waves, the wind in the trees, and the insects chirping in the jungle. And by a low, bloodcurdling howl that floated towards them from the inner jungle.

A second voice joined the howl, then a third, then more and more, louder and stronger. A chorus of canine voices, baying at the full moon as it rose over the water.

In that moment, Buck McLusky knew how Moon Bay had got its name.

Wolves! The ancient enemy of his breed! He could feel the fur on the back of his neck sticking up. He raised his head and stared into the jungle. A procession of figures, tall and lean and grey, was slinking down the beach towards them. They held burning torches in their paws, and their heads were lifted in song. Howl was answered by howl, a fresh voice taking up the note every time it began to falter.

Something stirred in McLusky's breast, and it was all he could do not to join in the wild, ancient music. *No!* He was a civilised dog—a protector of the weak, the innocent, and, frankly, those who just weren't as brave, smart, and talented as he was.

The wolves padded closer. Their leader was the tallest, standing silver in the moonlight, with a furless scar running across his chest and shoulder.

"*Run!*" barked McLusky. He grabbed the Dog Rose's paw. She pulled it away.

The two dogs pelted across the sand together. Behind them came the thud of furry feet as the wolf pack gave chase. The moon made a silver pathway across the ocean, but they couldn't escape that way. The jungle inland was too thick, and the wolves would know it too well. Out in the open they were more vulnerable, but maybe they could outrun the pack.

With his heartbeat hammering in his ears, and the Dog Rose panting beside him (and, he admitted, a little ahead of him). McLusky felt alive. There really was nothing like the thrill of the chase.

Too bad he was on the receiving end, rather than the chasing end.

The howls behind them were growing fainter. McLusky allowed his tail to wag a little. Wait . . . *that* howl had come from *in front* of them! The wolves had spread out to surround and trap them. He realised that the whimpering sound in his ears was coming from his own muzzle, and he clamped both paws over it as he ran.

"Cold feet?" mocked the Dog Rose. He was about to deny it, but she was right—his feet *were* cold. Silvery seawater washed over his white toes. The tide was coming in.

The wolfsong changed in pitch and cadence, becoming more urgent and excited. McLusky glanced around. They would be trapped against the cliffs by the tide, drowned or smashed against the rocks, unless they could outrun both nature and the pack to gain safety. What wouldn't he give to be back in civilisation—or at least to have a nice, civilised gun in his paws?

The water was up to his knees now. Little fish bumped against his legs, and weeds snagged his hind claws. He slipped on rocks, cutting the pads of his feet, but he kept going.

"McLusky." The Dog Rose tugged at his tail. "McLusky! It's no good, boy. They've got us."

"Get out!" boomed the wolf leader. "Get out or drown!"

Obediently, they stepped from the sea and allowed the wolves to lead them up the steep and winding path to the top of the cliffs. McLusky stumbled on the uneven ground, and the nearest wolf poked him in the back with her speartip. The water lapped far below them. The wolves raised their voices in a new song of savage triumph that made McLusky shiver. His ears folded over, and his tail tucked itself between his legs.

Wait, what was he doing? This wasn't behaviour befitting the beloved hero of the Dog Watch! He wasn't bred to be captured by wolves. He was bred to face them and drive them away, no matter how great the odds against him. To protect the innocent. Or, in this case (he glanced at the Dog Rose), the not so innocent.

"You'll never take me alive!" he declared. "I challenge you! Yes, you!" He pointed to the great, scarred leader.

"Very well," growled the wolf. His ears and muzzle were longer than McLusky's, he was grey all over, and his tail waved behind him rather than curling up. For McLusky, it was like looking into the face of his ancestor.

The husky's skills might have been honed in aerial dogfights, but he still had his fists and his teeth. He took a step backwards, dropping into a fighting stance.

His foot found air.

McLusky tried to recover, spinning his arms, but the cliff edge crumbled beneath him and he dropped into nothingness. He had always known it would end like this: the deadly fall, the hungry sea. He'd just assumed there would be a plane involved.

Something thumped into his chest so hard it knocked the breath out of him in a low *woof*. Claws dragged along his ribs and poked him in the eyes. He was under attack from—a bush? A bush! Thorny branches held him up as stones dislodged by his fall tumbled past, hitting the dark water so far below he couldn't hear the splashes. Saved, at least for now.

His wiggling toes found a crack in the rock. He felt his way along it as it widened enough for him to wedge his knee into the gap. He made himself release the bush and inch sideways. The gap became a ledge, and he dropped onto it.

He heard voices far above him, the Dog Rose calling his name, but he ignored them. He was no use to the Dog Rose if he was recaptured. He pressed himself back against the rock, and felt it give.

McLusky scrabbled at loose stones with his paws to reveal a hole in the cliff face. The entrance was narrow and dark, but it was a way of escape. He would go forward, no matter how difficult the path. Outwit the wolves, rescue the Dog Rose, and get them both out of there.

He brought out his regulation lighter and headed into the tunnel.

The rocks scraped his knees and the pads of his paws. There wasn't room to stand up, and at times he had to crawl on his belly or scrabble fallen rocks away. When he forced his head and shoulders through a tight squeeze, he tried not to think about whether or not he could get back if the passage tightened too much. There was only forward.

The blackness became grey, and he snapped the lighter shut. He made out a pale circle ahead: an exit! He shuffled forward, his tongue dry with chalk dust.

Cautiously, McLusky poked his muzzle into the light. He blinked, and, as his eyes slowly adjusted, he took in the scene. He was halfway up the wall of a vast, hollow chamber in the rock. Below him, the wolves were gathered around a fire, their primordial forms menacing in the flickering light. Where was the Dog Rose? What were they doing, these monsters? He looked closer. They were . . . grilling fish.

It smelled good.

His elbow knocked a pebble and he watched it bounce down the rock wall to the ground. Wolf ears flicked, and faces turned upwards.

"Come down here," boomed the wolf leader, baring his teeth. "Carefully, mind! Made that mistake when I was a pup, ha ha!" he added. He clapped a paw to the scar across his torso.

McLusky pulled himself out of the tunnel and scrambled down the rocks, landing in a heap in front of the leader.

"Well?" the big wolf asked, turning to the Dog Rose. "What shall we do with him?"

McLusky stood, brushed himself down, and looked around. Now he noticed the piles of treasure stacked around the chamber: squeaky toys, rubber balls of all sizes and colours, collars, ancient bones suffused with the exciting smells of ages past.

"You're in league with them!" McLusky burst out.

"You really are a bonehead, aren't you?" The rough collie put her paws on her hips. "We're not 'in league'. It's called being friends."

Now McLusky saw the dogs in flying gear mingling among the wolves wearing their natural fur. The pirates' hideout, at last. Protected from discovery by the rumours of savages, for who would risk landing at Moon Bay?

"We just wanted to give you a fright and get rid of you," continued the Dog Rose. "But you had to play the hero, didn't you? We thought you'd killed yourself! And now you know everything! What *are* we going to do with you?" Her voice became a growl, and her fangs showed.

"Now he's here," suggested the wolf leader, "I suppose we'd

better feed him."

McLusky gnawed the last of the flesh from a fishbone and licked his lips.

"I was wrong about you, Dog Rose. You're bad to the bone."

"Better than being a lickspittle lapdog."

"'Lickspittle'? Seriously? You're nothing but a thief. What do you even want with all this stuff?"

The Dog Rose removed a tennis ball from a carefully stacked pyramid, and bounced it. In spite of himself, McLusky's eyes followed the ball.

"It's the fun of acquiring it," she grinned.

"I'm going to make you give it all back."

"Even if I told you we drop it off anonymously to orphan pups who've never had a toy of their own before?"

"I don't believe you."

"If you can afford an airship cruise, you can afford to replace your knickknacks. We harm nobody. Just shake 'em up a bit. Give them something to brag about down at the Kennel Club."

Her fur was matted from the day's adventures, but McLusky could see how soft and lustrous it would be, brushed and groomed in a salon.

"You could be in the Kennel Club yourself," he told her. "You're a pedigree. Stunning. Society would love you. Why throw all that away for a life of crime?"

She grinned. "Crime? Or the life a dog should be leading? Hunting, living by your wits, taking risks? I couldn't stand to be spoiled and petted like those good boys and girls on the *Cavalier King Charles*. Sometimes we all need to be reminded there's a world beyond stuffy drawing-rooms and newer, squeakier squeaky toys and luxury airships!" Her brown eyes shone with passion. McLusky felt as if he had a tennis ball jammed in his throat.

The smoke from the fire was drawn upwards, disappearing through a hole in the rock roof. As the night passed, the full moon moved in its orbit until it was framed by the aperture.

The Dog Rose leaned closer. "There's a wolf inside all of us, Buck McLusky," she whispered in his ear. "You more than most. Find him!"

The wolf leader, sitting cross-legged by the embers, began a low howl. His pack added their voices, from the shrill yelps of the youngest cubs to the carrying note of the adults, and the Dog Rose, too, harmonised in a minor key.

McLusky gave in to the tickle at the back of his throat, closed his eyes, and joined in the song.

As the last notes died away, he blinked and shook himself. The Dog Rose was smiling at him, tricoloured fur hanging loose around her dark, mysterious eyes.

"Don't you get tired of doing the same thing every day? Defending the idle rich? Don't you want a new adventure? Stay here," she offered. "Stay."

McLusky wavered. The idea of getting rescued by some grinning junior officer of the Dog Watch, and then filing a report, suddenly seemed tiring. They'd laugh at him, think he'd lost his touch, start dropping hints about his retirement. Maybe he should simply disappear, leaving behind a legend. End his days swimming, dozing in the sun, and eating fish.

Then he thought of the airship captain relying on McLusky to restore his honour, and of the passengers, so sad without their trinkets. The instinct in him to chase had turned into a desire to guard and protect.

"I'm an old dog to be learning new tricks," he told her. "Besides, I love what I do. I'm an idol to millions and I strike fear into the heart of crooks. I protect the weak and innocent. And, if I may say so," he looked around at the gathering, "you and your friends don't look in need of my protection."

"Very well." The Dog Rose reached into her pocket. "You can take this little guy back to his owner. Tell him he had a good adventure."

McLusky took the toy kitten. "So did I."

"You won't give away our hideout?"

"No. Because then you'd get caught and put behind bars, and I enjoy chasing you too much to let that happen." McLusky wagged his curly tail. "And one day . . . one day, I'll catch you."

The Dog Rose leaned forward and kissed his cheek. "One day . . . I'll *let* you."

Tōrvi, Viking Queen

Melanie Marttila

I RAISE MY nose to the wind. Storm's coming. A good match for the one forming on deck. I huff in warning. And again, for attention.

I survey my shipboard pack as they ship their oars and stand, meeting each crewmember's eyes in turn. Most meet my gaze and then lower their heads in respect. Some look away, the curs. Fenris pants benignly but doesn't show respect.

"Who am I?" I bark.

"Torvi! Beloved of Thor!"

"Who *am* I?"

The response is more chaotic this time. Some bark, "Captain!" Others howl, "Queen!" Someone growls, "Meanest bitch on the sea!"

"Have I brought you to new lands?"

"Yes!"

"Have I seen your bellies filled with the choicest meats, the tenderest marrow?"

"Yes!"

"Have I won you steel claws?"

"Yes!" They draw and raise them in salute.

"Have one of you had to paddle for shore?"

"No!"

"Then who challenges my leadership?"

The pack falls to sniffing and grumbling. Fenris' hackles rise and the other canid back away from him.

"I do."

"Why?"

His panting and hackles fight with each other, mean to confuse, but I smell the intent beneath it all.

He puts one paw forward. "Meat and marrow and steel claws are all fine things, Torvi, but there are finer still."

"What is finer than the survival of our pack?" Not only our sea-going pack. I point to the crates of smoked and dried meats and bones we bring home to our families at the end of each voyage, the steel claws we give them for defence.

Fenris takes another step. "Silver, gold, and gems. We should raid the homin lands. Then, we can trade for all the meat and steel we want. And more, besides."

"What more do we need?"

He turns to address the crew. "Stone to build better homes. Meat animals so we won't need to hunt."

"You want us to trade warm and cosy dens for houses of cold stone? To become *farmers*?" I huff and my flews quiver, but no one else laughs. I appeal to my crew. "Do you want to become farmers?"

Several won't raise their heads. Enough to support Fenris' challenge? But even if this doesn't end in mutiny, my trust in my crew is shaken. The pack will break. I can't continue with crew I can't trust to have my back.

"If you want a homin life, with homin riches and houses, Fenris, you're welcome to go to their lands and take anyone who thinks the same with you. Go! Live with the homins. But you will not have this ship. And I will not sail to their shores on your behalf."

As I speak, Fenris turns to me, steps forward again. He's close enough to attack with claw and tooth, or steel. My paws itch to draw my weapons.

The wind has risen, driving the rain before it. The ship begins to roll with the waves.

"Who says that decision is yours to make?" Fenris tenses, though he still pants, his hackles still bristle.

"We are canid, proud hunters on land and sea. The pack is all, but the pack is led. If you are no longer satisfied with my leadership, you must express it. As a pack. Who is dissatisfied with all I have provided? Step forward."

Again, the crew fall to snuffling and shifting. Who among them will dare side with Fenris? Their howling support feels hollow, now, a distant pretence. Thunder rolls in the distance, sounds like doom.

A third move forward to stand with Fenris. He will not win the ship, but the damage is done.

My hackles rise, now. I look down at Fenris. Lightning flashes. Fortuitous timing. "The pack has spoken, Fenris, and not in your favour. Will you stand down, agree to leave this ship and pack with your sympathisers when we reach our homeland?"

"No."

"I will not make you swim for shore. I will not cage or chain you, but I can no longer trust you and you cannot remain part of this crew."

Fenris leaves off panting, finally, and growls.

"Do you still challenge me, Fenris? Is it your wish to fight?"

"It is."

The crew makes space on the deck for our combat. A rough circle of canid forms.

"Then choose the weapons we will use."

Fenris unbuckles the belt that holds his steel claws and tosses it well outside the ring. "Will tooth and claw suit your backward sensibilities?"

"They will." My blood is up. I remove my belt and discard my steel claws. I have no desire to kill Fenris, though, despite the trouble he's caused. His death would be a waste.

We step into the ring.

"Keille," I call to one of my faithful crew. "Though we meet not on a holm, this is yet a holmgang. Tell us what happens."

"If Torvi falls, Fenris must deliver half this ship's cargo to her pups and denmates in compensation. If Fenris falls, there is no debt, but he will be forever known as a canid whose bark is worse than his bite."

"We begin," I bark.

As if in omen, the storm breaks over us. Thunder sounds before the flash of lightning fades.

Fenris and I leap toward one another, teeth bared, claws flexed to strike.

Around us, the crew stomps on the deck, and then barks in low voices, keeping time. Stomp. Wuff. Stomp. Wuff.

I dodge Fenris' first blow, tackle low. Once he's down—but he won't fall. Sturdy cur.

Roll, regain my feet. But Fenris pushes his advantage. He's on top of me. Hot breath in my face. Sharp gust of snapping jaws. He won't get my throat. Draw my hind paws up to his gut. Kick. Kick. Kick.

Stomp. Wuff. Stomp. Wuff.

Flash. Rumble.

He reels back and I follow on. Dive on top. Avoid his kicks. Pin him down.

He howls.

Flash-rumble.

Stomp. Wuff. Stomp. Wuff.

My teeth at his throat. I bear down, wait for Fenris to go limp. He does not.

The ship rises on a swell, and we go rolling. I lose my hold. "Don't make me kill you."

"Give me the ship, and you won't have to."

We tumble against the gunwale, crew scrambling, almost go over.

Stomp. Wuff. Stomp. Wuff.

"We should be raising the tarps, bailing. The ship will founder and then neither of us will have her."

"Tarps and bailing. I'll be sure to do that," Fenris says as he pushes me into the sea.

I bite, latch onto his leathers, take him with me.

The howls of the crew follow us down.

Water closes over my head, flows into my mouth. I release Fenris, fight to find air.

I've barely gasped when I'm pulled down again. Fenris. Still don't want to kill him. Don't want to die, either. Fighting in water is challenging. Under it, almost impossible. No power to my blows. Still. Kick. Scratch. Bite.

I'm free, but I've lost the surface.

A bash to my head. Under the ship? An oar!

I sink my teeth into the wood. Trust my crew.

"—ot 'er," someone says when the oar brings me up.

Scramble aboard when the crew pull me in, wheeze water, vomit, brace and shake. It's almost as wet in the ship, though. Storm's in full force.

"Got him, too."

When I regain my breath, I bark, "Tarps and bailing, or we all swim!"

The crew set to.

Fenris lands on the boards with a soggy squelch.

"Leave off your foolishness. We've a ship and crew to save."

When they open, Fenris' eyes are black and bleak.

WE REACH HOME three days later, and Fenris and his supporters debark with their tails tucked and ears back.

It was a near thing, the storm. We have the ship, and we have our lives, but half our cargo was lost or spoiled. We needed every paw to save what we have. None of what's left will go to Fenris.

He turns to me and growls. "I will build my own ship and raid the homin lands. You'll see. I will be a king among canid. You will lower your head to me."

I sense the crew gathering at my back on the dock. "You forget. We do not have kings. Only queens. Still. Fare well on your quest." I raise my nose to the breeze, scent my pups before I see them. They're coming to welcome me home.

And I howl. "Who am I?"

"Torvi, beloved of Thor!" the crew howls.

"Who *am* I?"

"Queen Torvi!"

UNDER THE CURSE OF JUPITER

MATHEW AUSTIN

A WAVE ROSE from the sea, making the *Jupiter* look like a dinghy. It loomed over, blocking the sun, the crest forming a row of glimmering teeth. The jaw bit down, thundering into the deck and sweeping Montague overboard. They had sailed together since they were pups, cabin cubs for Sparkling Jack during his ill-fated journey down the Sturgeon's Pass. They had come through that unscathed, as well as his trips across Malagan's Cove, the Cape of Cornette, and the Battle of Churchill where old Jack danced a merry jig from his yardpaw. But here, a storm that had begun with only a smattering of rain, had doused Montague's flame in a blink and Hacker knew he would not be mourned, no good Boatswain was. Another wave flowed across the ship taking six more seadogs with it.

Fighting against the wind, Hacker pulled his way up the quarterdeck until he was face to face with the main mast. It creaked in time with the rocking of the ship but showed no sign of damage. "Mr. Godspeed." Hacker could feel his throat scratch as he bellowed through the speaker. "What can you see?"

"It's the same, Captain." Godspeed leaned over the edge of the crow's nest with daring and skill that Hacker rightly took for granted. "No end in sight."

"Carry on, Mr. Godspeed." Hacker cursed his luck. What had he done to enrage Pusseidon? He'd paid his dues, sacrificed blood and rum overboard, all to appease a God that seemed set on vengeance for a wrong not committed.

"What should we do, Captain." Lockheed's ears were pasted to the side of his head and his shaggy mane drooped with the weight of water, yet the Sailing Master still had his toothy yellow smile and the pigeon feathers in his hat.

"Keep her straight and true, Mr. Lockheed. Let the seacat scratch, this old ship can take it."

TANTO TALKED DRIVEL when he was drunk, tales so tall that not even the dullest fool would have given them credence. Yet it was different when he was dying and as he bled claret onto Hacker's best evening shirt, there seemed to be a sincerity in his glassy eye. "Don't move, don't move," Hacker had said, but deep down he wanted his jaw to keep yapping.

"You ain't seen nothing like it. There's more treasure than earth in that there land. We's would have got the lot, but captain he says it's too hot. Let it cool, he said, but now we're all cold, even me."

"You'll be all right, Tanto, a scurvy dog like you ain't dying from a small poke in the gut." Tanto laughed, grimaced, and coughed blood onto Hacker's cheek. "Easy, easy."

"You's a good bark, Hacker. That lot o' cutthroats, they wouldn't make it but you's know how to sail. You's like my ol' captain." Tanto reached into his pocket and pulled out a scruffy piece of catskin. "Take this and say nay a word to a soul lest you wish to hit an early kennel like this ol' timer here. And when you find those stones, you dig, sonny, o' you dig."

Hacker wished he had never dragged Tanto out of that bar, if he had left him to the wolves it would have been some other fool staring down a crew that was looking for answers right now. He had two mates, eight seadogs, and an officer all drinking tea with Davey Bones and not a ducat or a dogbloon to show for it. No barkaneer feared the tip of a cutlas, the crash of a cannon, or the hangman's noose, they were all part and parcel of business, but a seadog died for treasure, not a dream. And dream is what this was. A foolish dream that preyed on Hacker's weakness for adventure.

Looking out across his crew he knew that most of them had fallen into piracy; when one couldn't earn, they took, and when they took enough, they got a taste for it. Hacker was different to the rest of them, there had been other paths he could have walked, ones that came with titles and honour, but he had chosen the pirate's way. "Axel Abbott, Buzz Cain, Flash Duke," he began, his paws behind his back and his eyes holding all in place, "Freddy Bannister, Gunner Jackson, Jasper Hutt, Lucky Stansfield, Quincy Porter, Spot Rockwell, Shadow Piper, and Scout Montague." He took the bicorne from his head, held it over his heart, and all before him did the same.

"May their waters forever be calm and winds always be strong. May their stomachs be full and their coffers overflowing. May they sail in peace." He paused as they chanted the tragic line back to him. "Every seadog lost was a barkaneer at heart. None shook duty when it lay before them and none dishonoured their name. Each knew why they were here, each dreamed bigger than your average freebooter and threw in their pennies for the chance to get their paws dipped in gold. They died in the pursuit of that dream. When we hit the shores of fortune, make certain their names are echoed in the halls of your hallowed homes, so all know what price the crew of the *Jupiter* was willing to pay for a chance at immortality. Tonight each of you gets an extra strip of rum and if I don't hear you singing their names, there won't be a dog on board who isn't food for Pusseidon. May they sail in peace!" He screamed and they screamed back.

CAPTAIN HACKER HAD no taste for luxuries. His cabin was nothing but wood and hard corners. He had journeyed enough to know that opulence sunk ships faster than cannon balls. Gold hungry dogs lost their appetite when wealth was just behind a captain's door, the pledge of loyalty easily undone by the allure of shiny metal. "A captain is meat when he forgets his crew is nothing more than thieves," Anne Boney had told him one summer at a convention in Porta Looga. "Trust them with your life, but never with your back." Hacker thought about the looks that had been on their faces this day as he lay down on his cot. They would sing tonight and they would work tomorrow, but the day after that he could not be certain.

Before he had a chance to close his eyes, there was a knock on the door. "Enter."

The door opened and Sickert poked his head around. "Now a good time, Sir?" Hacker waved him in. The Quartermaster was dressed in his finest doublet and his fur was combed straight. There had been some that said Bingo Sickert was too pretty to sail, but those mutts were dead and Sickert hadn't even dirtied his clothes doing it. "We need to talk about a new Boatswain."

"Stansfield, was his apprentice?" Sickert nodded. "What about Ringo Peeps? Lad has a fine head on his shoulders and reads about as well, or should I say badly, as Montague did."

"Cook won't spare him."

"Well, tell the cook he either spares the boy or we'll be eating him for tomorrow's supper." Hacker took two mugs and a bottle from beneath his desk. He poured a dram in each and handed a mug to Sickert. "To Monty," he said and they both drank. "You know Monty hated water. Loved the sea, but hated being wet. He almost lost his mind when Sparkling Jack scuttled us off the coast of Calypso and he had to paddle to shore in nothing but his britches. Still, Monty was the first with his hand up when the next job came around. We won't find another like him either on board or at any port from here to Christendom." There was another knock at the door and cabin-pup Bates appeared with a tray. "Lay it down," Hacker said and the young 'un put it on the desk. "Would you let Mister Lockheed know I wish to see him as soon as is convenient?"

"Aye aye, Captain." Bates saluted and ran out the cabin.

"Change of course?" Sickert asked once the door slammed shut.

"Something like that." Instinct made Hacker tap his breast pocket where Tanto's map resided and rarely ever left. He had shown it to none, fearful of the consequences should the crew discover that they were led by a map as vague as the snow was white.

"I shall leave you to you supper." Sickert straightened his collar in the mirror as Hacker removed the lid from his bowl. Steam rose from broth the colour of sputum, as lumps of dried liver bobbed like driftwood. Hacker sunk in his spoon and brought it to his lips. "Stop!" Sickert ran and smacked the spoon out of his hand. "Can't you smell it? What good is your nose if you never bother to use it." Hacker leaned over the bowl and sniffed.

He stood up straight, wide-eyed and sweating at the distinctive scent of chocolate.

CAPTAIN HACKER WALKED back and forth across the quarter deck as Lockheed pulled the ship three klicks starboard. The sail swelled and the *Jupiter* cut through fog and choppy water in search of new lands. The crew scrambled across the deck, pulling, shouting, lifting, there was not an idle paw to be seen. It was a sight that used to make Hacker happy, but now he knew there was a killer in their midst.

Sure, they were all murderers in the eyes of the law and God, the only certainty in life was a noose or damnation, but a pirate killed with the point of his cutlas or the ball in his gun, not with poison in soup. "All correct, Captain." Lockheed smiled at him and Hacker tried to deduce if the Sailing Master was genuine. Lockheed had been steering him true and proper for as long as he was issuing orders, he was the sort of seadog that prioritised adventure over ambition. That was what Hacker's instinct was telling him, and out at sea, a captain without an instinct might as well be a corpse in the water.

"Very good, Mr. Lockheed. Alert me to any change."

"Aye aye, Captain."

"Captain Hacker," a voice called. Blackjack Sampson's head protruded from the foredeck hatch. He looked grim but the old pug always did, the years of fighting having left him more scars than skin.

"What is it, Blackie?"

"You's wanted in the stores, Captain."

"The helm is yours, Mr. Lockheed." Down in the bowels of the ship, he passed mutts offering bows and nods and noted the good order of the sleeping quarters. He had been on many ships where below the deck it went to the cats, but Hacker held the *Jupiter* to a different standard; they were professionals, not amateurs, and it was only when the crew boarded a prize that they were allowed to become cutthroats.

As ordered, Buckman stood in front of the armoury, his back ridged but his head on a swivel. Hacker had pulled Buckman out of fires and flames, bringing him aboard the *Jupiter* where a man betrayed by his own had found comfort amongst those he had once hunted. He was as loyal as the day was long, although now it seemed like the sun was forever on the verge of setting. "Any problems, Mr. Buckman?" he asked the old black-eyed boxer.

"No, Sir."

"Carry on."

"Thank you, Sir."

Down past the keel and the hold they found the storeroom shut up tight, Sickert leaning against the door. "They're in there. You don't really think either of them did it, do you?"

"Someone did and I'm not going to wait for them to do it again." Hacker pushed open the door and found the cook and cabin-pup Bates sitting on sacks of potatoes.

"What this all about, Captain?" the cook said. Hacker looked for a sign of guilt, but did not even find a raised hair.

"Well, Mr. Becker, Mr. Bates, we find ourselves in quite a predicament." Hacker took off his hat and sat down on a barrel of salt. "Today I had the misfortune of finding my supper to be spiked with chocolate." They both began to talk but he held up a paw for silence. "Fortunately, Mr. Sickert's nose is second to none. Had he not been there I may very well right now be making acquaintance with the seabed. Someone wants me dead and unfortunately, gentlemen, right now evidence points at one of you."

"Captain, I would never—"

"I don't want to hear how you would never," Hacker leaned forward and snarled, "I want to hear how you didn't. Convince me it wasn't you and maybe I won't have to walk anyone up the plank. And, gentlemen, be frank and forthcoming or you'll be talking to Blackie instead of me."

The two accused recoiled and Blackjack pulled a piece of cloth from his pocket and slowly wrapped it around his right paw. A prize pug, he had fought a hundred fights, each one a bloody, brutal affair, but at the end he had had his arm raised whilst his opponent lay unmoving on the ground. He had come to sea for a quiet life, but Hacker knew that old fire still burned inside him.

The chef and Bates talked over each other, a stream of unintelligible babble, and once again Hacker called for silence. "Enough! One a time. Mr. Becker, you begin."

"It was like any other day, Captain . . ." the cook prided himself on his cuisine and walked them through the evening's minutia: how he had seasoned the liver, making sure the captain received the chucks that still had some colour; how he'd picked vegetables free from mould and baked bread the texture of rock. "I served yours first, because I always think of you first and then I handed it to Bates. Why would I bring chocolate aboard? It's madness, Sir."

"What say you, Mr. Bates?" The cabin-pup raised his head, took one look at Blackjack, and returned his gaze to the floor. "You may be little more than a pup, Mr. Bates, but you'll hang like any old bark, so pick your head up and get to talking."

"C-c-captain . . ."

"Head up!" Bates' head rose, his eye dripping sea water. "Speak your piece, lad."

"Well, C-captain . . . it was as Cook says, it was any other day . . ." Bates' story was short and simple. He answered the cook's call, a howl that could prick up the ears of even the deepest sleeper. He hurried down, no stop along the way, and watched as the cook spooned hot liver and broth into a bowl.

"And then what?"

"Then I covers it with the lid and I brings it up to you, Captain. No one stops me, I came straight there . . . I wish there was more, but that's the truth of it." Bates' head fell back down. Hacker had not expected a confession. He wanted to believe them, but the only thing lies could not hide from was pain. Their stories rang true and the thought of torturing innocent dogs nagged at him. A ship's life was one of repetition, days and weeks disappeared without change, yet the best lies were rooted in reality. "Why would I want to kill you, Captain," Bates whimpered, "it makes no sense."

Why would they want to kill me? All actions had a justifiable reason, and there was not one he could think of. *Kill me?* Hacker's eyes expanded, and he pulled Sickert down by his collar, whispered in his ear, and the Quartermaster set off at breakneck speed.

"Captain?" Blackjack said, stepping forward.

"Not yet, Blackie." No one spoke and Hacker set his paws together in front of his lips. The door swung open and Sickert returned, panting.

"All of it . . . the whole thing . . . half the crew . . . maybe more."

Hacker stood up. "Mr. Becker, where do you store the liver?"

"Over there, Captain." The cook pointed to a wood barrel in

the corner. Hacker pried off the lid and Sickert put his head inside. He came up and nodded. "Call all paws to the deck, Mr. Sickert."

"What's going on, Captain?"

"It appears your liver has been spiked, Mr. Becker. The whole crew has been poisoned."

THE SURGEON GRIMACED and scratched at his cheek; there were fleas going around, but Hacker knew that was not what gnawed at him. "Fifteen showing symptoms, eight chronic, and I'd say half of those are dead before the night is out."

"And what of the rest of the crew?"

"Most ate it, but it seems to be luck o' the draw. Lockheed had the helm, so at least we'll still be sailing straight. It could be worse."

Hacker did not share the Surgeon's sentiment. A ship without paws was a ship as good as sunk. Add to the mix that there was a saboteur on board and it was turning out to be a bad day. "Thank you, Mr. Shortcake." The Surgeon nodded and left the cabin. "Speak your mind, Bingo." He had watched Sickert bite his claws through the Surgeon's report. The Quartermaster was never short on words unless he had something tough to say and it looked like he was chewing pebbles.

"Well, Sir . . ."

"Out with it."

"Captain, I have never doubted or swayed in my faith in your plan. Adventure and mystery are as much a pirate's calling as gold and rum, and the barkaneer in me says carry on into the great unknown, let this ragtag band of misfits prove to all that they are a cut above. That what the bark in me says, but the part of me that's an officer has to listen to his head not his heart. We know what's behind us and embarrassing though it may be, it's better to come back into port with one's tail between the legs than to have no tail at all."

The pebbles were hard to swallow, but Sickert was only putting into words what Hacker already knew. When a dream became a nightmare, all one could do was wake up and, tired though he may be, Hacker's eyes were wide open. He looked at the hat that hung from a nail on the cabin wall. He had inherited it when he had first assumed command of the *Jupiter*, a rite of passage after the passing of old Pickled-Jim; it had had never sat snug and wobbled in the wind. "Would you please summon the Sailing Master to my quarters?"

"Aye aye, Sir."

Sickert reached for the handle but the door swung open. Lockheed stood in the threshold, his white fur standing on end and chill blowing through the doorway. "Captain, you must come."

EVERY PIRATE FEARED a cursed ship yet none had sailed one. Tales were told, but they were third paw accounts; no seadog came back from a cursed ship alive. As Hacker stared through his spyglass, he continued to wonder what great wrong he had committed. It had gone beyond Pusseidon's wrath; this was vengeance straight from the great dog in the sky. Nothing froze a barkaneer's blood like a Portuguese dog-o'-war with its twenty gun broadside and giant sails that seemed to spit wind. It was a terrier-of-the-seas, it made the *Jupiter* look like a sloop in a fleet of frigates. "Any sign she's seen us?"

Godspeed shook his head. "Not whilst this fog lasts, but it'll clear by daybreak."

Hacker collapsed the spyglass and returned it to his pocket. "Carry on, Mr. Godspeed." Descending from the crow's nest, his paws worked whilst his brain focused on other things and only when he hit the deck did he return to the present.

"Well?" Sickert asked.

"As big and mean as they come. How much of a head start would we need, Mr. Lockheed?"

"More than we'll get, Captain, she'd swallow us whole in under an hour."

"Dowse the lamps and hold the fog for as long as you can. Mr. Sickert, my quarters." Hacker carried a lantern to his cabin as the rest of the ship fell victim to black of night. He placed it on the desk as Sickert drew the blinds of the stern-side window. "Take a seat, Bingo." Sickert sat on the cot whilst Hacker paced the room. "We're in a might bit of trouble here."

"Aye, what we did to deserve this I don't know."

"I thought the same. Have you ever heard of such rotten fortune?"

"Not in all my years. There will be talk of a curse soon."

"There will." Hacker nodded and tapped his claws on the desk. "When one thing goes wrong it's bad luck, two things even worse, but three . . ."

"Are you suggesting someone has a paw in this?"

"Precisely." A dog of the sea did not believe in a script. One fought elements and obstacles, and survival was a matter of skill, not fate. There was no such thing as a doomed voyage, just adventures that were only meant for top-dogs. If an undertaking was damned from the beginning it was because someone was meddling. Storms occurred and mutinies took place, but warships did not wander into uncharted waters. "Someone has overplayed their paw."

"Our saboteur?"

"Undoubtably." Hacker scratched behind his ear. "What is the sensible course of action in this situation?"

"Hoist the white and pray for mercy, I suppose."

"And will we find any?"

"Not for us, no."

"And not for any other soul onboard. The lucky ones will be tossed in the drink and the rest of us will be dragged through hell and high water just to be fodder for the hangdog. And yet the situation calls for submission." Hacker forced a smile. "I once shared a meal with Calico Jack Russell. Jack wasn't like the rest of us, too well-spoken, too well-mannered, and not all that interested in gold; but his crew loved him, no more loyal in all the world. Jack said to me that 'a captain is the one that overcomes what no other can, so until one pulls victory from the jaws of defeat, you're a dog in a hat eating the best cuts of meat.' Our dog in the shadows wants us to surrender, so let's show him that logic and lunacy are cut from the same cloth."

"HOIST THE WHITE." The torn piece of sheeting rose to the top of the ship as the fog cleared the stern. "Toss anchor and single shot." A splash of water preceded the sound of a solitary cannon, that was the death rattle of any fighting vessel. The ocean rose and fell, and the frigate began its approach, eating water like chum. The *Jupiter* looked like the runt of the litter as the ship came alongside, and Hacker counted twenty-six guns pointed their way.

A figure in a blue uniform held a metal speaker to its mouth.

"In the name of His Faithful Majesty King Jonjo Braganza, we the crew of the *Cachorra* demand your surrender. Prepare to be boarded."

"In line, weapons down." The crew stood in formation behind Hacker, as pistols and cutlasses hit the deck. The captain unhooked his scabbard from his belt and held the sheathed sword in front of him. He had bought it in Porta Looga at a pop-up smithy that specialised in cutlery. The sword was nothing special, but had seen him through Churchill and more raiding parties than he could count and was not easily tossed away.

The rampway thudded down and the blue uniformed grunts came aboard, marching in perfect time. They parted to allow their captain through, a tall regal figure whose jacket was lined with buttons as gold as his fur. The epaulettes on his shoulders shook in the breeze and the bicorne on his head showed no signs of wear and tear. He approached with paws behind his back, stopping a yard in front of Hacker and eyeing him up and down.

His top lip curled upwards and exposed a perfect set of white teeth. "I'm Captain Hacker."

"I am aware who you once were." He took the sword and tossed it to a dog behind him. "Now you are merely criminals in the custody of Captain Dogrido Duarte. That is I."

"We surrender and appeal for mercy."

"Typical pirate. Always looking for something they would never dream of offering."

"We are criminals, you are gentlemutts."

"I see that even scum has an eye for refinement." Duarte looked beyond Hacker at the scant line of dogs behind him. "And where is the rest of your crew?"

"Chocolate outbreak, sickbay full to the brim." The captain showed no sign of surprise.

"I will, of course, be scouring this ship. And if I find that you have been lying to me, I will flay, burn, and drown your crew without a second thought. All except you, Hacker. You're food for His Majesty, come what may. Are we understood?"

"Perfectly."

"Sit." No one moved. "I said sit!" Hacker turned and nodded; the crew got down on their haunches. Duarte clicked his tongue and set off with Hacker walking behind him flanked by two guards who looked like they had seen more fights than dinners.

They delved down into the bowels of the *Jupiter*. It was silent other than the creaking of wood and the splashing of water, as hammocks hung empty and guns sat unprimed. The first signs of life came as they approached the sick bay, groans and heavy breathing emanating from behind the door. Hacker opened it, releasing a wave of putrid air. Barks lay on mats, their faces contorted in pain, a wall of canvas corpse bags mounted at the back of the room.

"Can I help you?" the Surgeon said, his white coat stained brown and red.

"Why are these dogs not topside?" Duarte's paw gripped the hilt of his sword.

"They can't be moved. Half of them are at death's door."

"I want them up now."

"But they'll die."

"Then they'll die. Up!"

"Please," Hacker took off his hat and held it in front of him, "if you want me to beg then I'll beg, just let sleeping dogs lie."

"Fine, then beg for me, boy."

Hacker got down on his knees, took a deep breath, and looked up at Duarte.

The captain grinned, his tail wagging as the cuckoo sang from the clock behind him. "Now, what do you say?"

"Boom."

"Boom?"

An explosion deafened all ears and the boat rocked from side to side. Hacker jumped to his feet and landed a hard right paw on Duarte's chin, sending him to the ground. The old sea dog jumped upon his fallen foe, biting and tearing at anything left exposed. The two guards moved to intercept, but turned their backs on the sick bay, allowing Blackjack and Buckman to rise from beneath their blankets. The Marines were no match for two old veterans and soon their blue uniforms were stained red.

"Get him in the brig, then head up topside," Hacker ordered, pointing at the fallen captain who whimpered for his mother.

Hacker unbuckled Duarte's sword and strapped it to his waist. He climbed the ladder with a cold precision, pushing the God-fearing canine to one side and raising up the hellhound inside of him. As he arrived on the deck, he was greeted by the kiss of a bayonet. He sidestepped the thrust and impaled his enemy with the tip of Duarte's sword. It was a flimsy piece of equipment, meant for decoration, not death, but it killed all the same, adding more blood to the ever-reddening deck.

Hacker was late to a party that was in full swing. Uniforms danced with ragged vests, the boys in blue dropping like flies. Sickert's raiding party was tearing through them from the starboard side, whilst plumes of fire shot up from the bowels of the *Cachorra*. The Captain and the Quartermaster locked eyes across the melee, and Sickert waved his bloodstained sword before cutting his way through the throng.

"Report."

"Smooth-as-silk, Captain. Just like clockwork."

Duarte had thought he had all the facts. He had not so much as blinked when he heard of the chocolate outbreak and walked the deck with the confidence of one who knew his opponent was beaten. Such confidence made a dog sloppy. So sloppy that a skiff-ful of mutts could hide in the fog, float unseen up to the side of the *Cachorra* and clamber in through her gun ports. A fire in the magazine, a blindside attack, and the battle was good as won.

"The deck is yours, Mr. Sickert. I would like you to bring me a head count after the boys have had their fun." Hacker headed towards his cabin. "Oh, and Bingo."

"Yes, Captain?"

"Find my sword for me, would you? I want a weapon, not a toothpick."

THE BUTCHER'S BILL was in and it was set to be a cheap Christmas. A few cuts and bruises and old Blakey would not be walking anytime soon, but none of the *Jupiter* had gone to meet their maker. The *Cachorra* had not been so lucky. What remained of her crew sat on the deck with their paws bound behind them, waiting for a pirate's justice. Their heads turned as Duarte was escorted up to the quarterdeck. His fur was torn and scruffy, his face swollen, his teeth chipped and he walked with a limp, each stride inducing a grimace. Hacker stood by the wheel, impassive as Duarte was placed in front of him.

"Do you want me to beg?" Duarte fell to his knees and looked up.

"Talking will suffice. I want the name of your source. Who told you where we would be?"

Duarte shook his head. "I have no idea what you speak of." Hacker turned his head and nodded to Buckman, who grabbed a prisoner by the lapels and threw him overboard. There was panic on deck, but the thoughts of rebellion were doused by the threat of cold steel.

"I will repeat. Who told you where we would be?"

"Querido Deus . . ." Duarte shook his head and Buckman sent another of the *Cachorra's* crew over the side of the ship. "Please!"

"I can keep asking this question, but sooner or later it'll be your turn."

"I don't know."

Hacker turned again, but felt a paw grab his leg.

"Please! I'm telling you, I don't know. I would get messages by bird, they told us where to go, said you would be here ripe for picking. The admiralty said follow instructions, I don't know where they came from. Please, you have to believe me."

"I do, Duarte, I do."

"Deus seja louvado." Duarte let go of Hacker's leg as the Captain gave Buckman the signal. The old wardog grabbed Duarte by the back of his collar and dragged him towards the edge. "But I told the truth!"

"You did, and that will save your crew, but not you."

THE CREW OF the *Cachorra* stood impassively on what remained of their ship as the *Jupiter* began to move away. "Think they'll make it?" Sickert asked Hacker.

"A seadog worth his salt finds his way home even if he has to swim."

"Captain." Blackjack Sampson stood in front of him with Badger Pereira at his shoulder.

"What is it, Blackie?"

"This here lad has something to say." He pushed Pereira forward. Pereira was little more than a welp yet to shed his first fuzz, but he had never shirked his duty and swung a sword as good as any. "Speak your piece, lad. Don't waste the Captain's time."

"It's like this, Captain . . ." A pup he may have been, but Pereira had done his time in the navy, mopping decks and stuffing guns. There was nothing special about his story, many of the crew had walked the same pathway, swapping order and duty for rum and gold. Hacker suppressed the urge to tell Pereira to hurry up. Storytelling was in a pirate's soul and a story told short was not worth telling at all. The light had begun to fade when Pereira got to the crux of his tale. He had served with one of the crew of the *Cachorra* and as all waited for Duarte to be brought topside, the two old friends had got to talking. Pereira's jaw moved as much as his paws, but this time he did most of the listening. Midshipman Bollo told of a journey that had been one disaster after the other. From stale water and rotten meat to an outbreak of fleas, nothing seemed to go right, they had even come becalmed off the coast of an island that did not appear on a map. "Now that got my ears pointing upwards, I can tell you."

"Did he say where?"

"Aye, a day southwest from 'ere. A whaling spot as good as any he said, so if you see them blowing you'll know you're heading true."

"You have earned yourself an extra strip of rum, Mr. Pereira."

"Thank you, Captain."

"Dismissed." Hacker closed his eyes and breathed in through his nose, saltwater fresh in his nostrils. "Mr. Lockheed." The Sailing Master looked up from the wheel. "Set a south-westerly course."

"Aye aye, Captain."

"Mr. Sickert." He walked with the Quartermaster to the starboard gunwale, the *Cachorra* little more than a speck in the distance. Hacker's knees were weak and if he closed his eyes he would sleep for a month. "This is it, Bingo."

"Are you sure?"

"It fits. My nose may not be as sharp as yours, but I can smell it."

WATER SHOT TEN foot into the air, as beasts from the deep glided past the *Jupiter's* bow. The crew looked on with slackened jaws. "Seacat's servants," the cook said. "Seems like ol' puss has got over her gripe."

"Land ho!" came a cry from the crow's nest and attention moved from the sea to the horizon. Hacker pulled his spyglass from his pocket and fastened it to his eye; through the round lens faint shapes became sand and rocks.

"All paws, prepare for disembark." The spell was broken and

the crew began to move. "Drop anchor." There was a distinctive splash and Hacker turned to Sickert. "I'm leaving my ship in your capable paws, I do hope you return her in one piece."

"I'll do my best not to sink her."

"Sorry to leave you behind."

"We all dream of being captain, even if it's just for an afternoon. Fame and fortune to you, Sir."

"Fame and fortune, Bingo." Hacker climbed down the side of the ship and landed aboard the *Ganymede*. The small skiff that had felled the *Cachorra* wobbled beneath him as he took his seat near the stern. "Mr. Lockheed, if you would get us underway." The Sailing Master shouted orders, oars hit the water, and the *Ganymede* began to move. Each stroke pulled in time with the beat of Hacker's heart. It thumped, getting steadily faster as the land crept closer. "Pull us to shore, lads." The crew jumped overboard and began dragging the small boat up onto the dark beige sand. Hacker could hear the scraping of the ground beneath the hull and held up his arm, and the boat came to a stop. He stepped onto the beach and almost fell. Dry land turned sober dogs into drunks, the steadiness of the ground unnatural to his sea-legs. He wobbled forward as his body slowly remembered what it was to be a landlubber.

"Captain?"

"A minute if you will, Mr. Lockheed." He pulled the map from his breast pocket, the sun lighting up the markings and scrawls of his old friend Tanto. Eyes burned into his back. This was the first the crew had seen of the mythical map, the item that had drawn them into the unknown and their friends to the bottom of the ocean. He held it in front of him as he walked forward up a sandy bank, over rocks and stone until he arrived at an expanse of overgrown grassland. The ground was hard beneath him and he stooped down and found a moss-covered square slab of stone. Hacker looked at the map and then back at the stone, a broad grin spreading across his face. "Onward, you no good seadogs! Fame and fortune doesn't wait for lollygaggers." They raised weapons and shovels in the air and howled to the sky, then the crew of the *Jupiter* began to move.

The stone path came and went. The map led them through trees and meadows, to the foot of a great hill. The sun burned the back of Hacker's neck as he climbed, breathing like an old hound, his tongue hanging out the side of his mouth. None broke step, all drawn upwards by what lay at the crest of the hill.

The top of the hill spread out into a wide plateau, at the centre of which were the ruins of a kennel, unlike any Hacker had seen before. Vast broken walls of yellow brick plunged deep into the earth, and a pair of arched wooden doors lay rotting on the ground. The ruin was surrounded by a series of stone obelisks each at least a dog-head high, etched with weathered markings written in no common tongue. Hacker stood in front of one and it cast a shadow over him, chilling the sweat on his spine. "Dig," he ordered, and the crew needed no more instruction.

Paws and shovels broke the earth and dirt flew in the air as they burrowed deep into the ground. Hacker stood and watched, his arms behind his back, his mouth dry like the morning after a night on the rum. No one spoke as the tension mounted like the banks of earth, until a loud hollow thud rang out and a voice cried, "Captain!" Hacker moved to the edge of the hole where his dogs were clearing dirt from the top of a long wooden box. Blackjack looked up at him, his eyes shining.

"Open it up."

The crew clambered out as the old pug dug his shovel into the side of the box and pushed downwards with gritted teeth, the muscles of his back breaking the seam of his shirt. There was a crack of wood, and Blackjack threw his shovel out of the hole and pulled the lid off of the box. A cloud of dust flew up into the air, blinding the onlookers.

"What is it?"

There was no reply.

"Blackie, what is it?"

The dust began to settle and Blackjack came back into view. "It's bones, Sir. It's full of bones!" Bones of all shapes and sizes lay in the box. Some were round, others long, some even had five smaller bones attached that wobbled when moved.

"Bones," Hacker whispered, and the word spread like fire amongst the crew, until a moment of brief silence and a roar of delight. "Bones! Have you ever seen so many bones in one place? Quick, boys, get to the rest of those stones. If my nose is right, we're in for the haul of a lifetime."

The barkaneers scattered across the hilltop, each finding a stone and scrabbling at the earth. One by one the cries rang out,

"Bones!" and a dog would scramble from the hole and move on the next stone.

Hacker calculated the cost of bones on the open market. Prices were already at an all-time high, but bones this size were as rare as hen's teeth and would have every dog drooling.

"Captain."

He looked over to see Lockheed waving him towards the ruined kennel.

"You must see this."

"What is it?" Hacker said, walking through crumbled remains of an archway.

"At the back, Sir." The captain walked deeper into the ruin until he heard a distinctive click. He turned round, a tiredness in his shoulders, and found himself staring at the barrel of a pistol.

"The wolf in our midst bares his teeth. So what's the plan here, Lockheed. Shoot me, then what?"

"Then you'll be dead."

"That I will and so will you. These boys will tear you limb from limb."

"These boys are buried with their heads in the earth. A small crack of powder won't carry over the wind."

"And then what?"

"And then I'll be at the *Jupiter*, with oh such a tail to tell."

"Sounds a far-fetched plan to me. I'd ask you why, but it's always gold isn't it?"

"Bones will fill your belly, but gold is why we live. Goodbye, Captain." There was a click, but no crack. Lockheed pulled the trigger for a second time and again nothing.

"Always pack your own powder. You have a gun full of sawdust." Hacker took his own pistol from his belt and pulled back the hammer. "You're slippery, Mr. Lockheed, but not subtle. You alone knew which way I wanted to sail my ship. I found it strange the enemy did too."

"You think—"

Hacker shot, Lockheed fell, and in the distance, someone cried "Bones."

THE *JUPITER* CRASHED through the water as the cry of "land ho!" came from the crow's nest. Porta Looga hovered in the distance and Hacker tried to hide his relief. A cursed journey had turned into a cruise. With the Jonah off her deck, the *Jupiter* moved with a serene peace, her belly full of plunder. Hacker was not a mathematician, but his rudimentary calculations left every dog aboard richer than they could have ever hoped.

"What will you do with your cut, Bingo?"

Sickert scratched at the fur of his chin. "I haven't had a proper drink or a glimpse of the fairer sex in close to a month."

"After the usual?"

"To tell you the truth, I hadn't given it much thought. You?"

"The hull could use a scrub."

They stood in silence as first sounds of civilisation hit the deck.

"You know, Sir. There was a rumour swirling that the wreck the *Concordia* was spotted off some rocks near the coast of No-Dogs Cove."

"Blackhart's old boat? Word had it Blackhart found the new world. Would be quite the prize if one could get a hold of his maps."

"It would indeed. Still, not much to go on."

Hacker nodded to himself. "Set sail in a month?"

"Aye aye, Captain."

THE BOOMER BUST

JB RILEY

"I DON'T WANT to be a pirate!"

I put on a bright smile and patted her shoulder. "Jocelyn, pirates are fun, you'll see. Plus, Captain Hook needs you. It's an important role and I know you'll do a great job dancing and singing 'yo ho ho'."

There was already a lot of 'yo-ho-ho'ing around us. Fifty or so assorted kids and dogs plus adults trying to keep them in rough groups of pirates, Indians, mermaids, and Lost Boys made quite a ruckus. I could hear Mrs. Gantry's piano in the next room only faintly, which was fine with me. One more practice round of "Tender Shepherd" and I just might scream.

Speaking of screaming, Jocelyn's face was turning bright pink as her voice got louder. "I don't *want* to be a pirate. Why can't I be Wendy?"

Because you couldn't carry a tune if I poured it into a bucket and handed it to you. "Well, honey, you know, it's Courtney's turn. She's been a Lost Boy, and a pirate, and now she gets to be Wendy. It's only fair."

Leaving the reluctant pirate to her pouting, I straightened and scanned the room.

Using the school's fall play for a "Furry Orphans" fundraiser was genius. Adding dogs to the show as some of the pirates and Lost Boys was also genius, at least in theory. In practice? Not so much.

Three students had to be recast for allergies, including the original John, whose eyes had swelled shut to the point the school nurse had an uncapped epi-pen ready in case the liquid Benadryl didn't kick in. Students couldn't learn their lines and songs and cues *and* keep track of the dogs so we had to add significantly to the cast. Between actors, dog handlers, stage crew, sets, ushers, ticket takers, concessions workers, and the small band Mrs. Gantry would oversee, virtually every student was involved. It was a massive undertaking for our little rural school.

Plus, it turned out Captain Hook was apparently a cat person.

"Lindsey! Lindsey Carlyle!"

Stifling an eye roll I turned around. "Yes, Professor?"

Johnathan—not "John," "Jack," or—heaven forfend—"Johnny"—Roche was coming toward me at full steam. Retired home to Decatur years ago from Loyola of Chicago's Theatre Department, he was a reliable volunteer and didn't flaunt his career (much) over my lowly grammar school teacher-ness. So long as the play's program included a full-page ad from students and staff thanking "Professor Emeritus Johnathan Roche, without whose invaluable efforts the show could not go on" or similar claptrap, he would play Captain von Trapp, The Wizard, Fagin, or any other role where an adult, male, and admittedly very good baritone was needed.

Right now, however, Hook looked unhappy. Pinching a tattered piece of cloth between two fingers, he held it up at arm's length and waved it. "Do you know what this is?"

"Umm . . ."

His nostrils flared above a slightly askew fake moustache. "This—" wave "—was—" wave "—my cravat. Before it was destroyed by one of these infernal canines." He flung both arms wide. "I cannot work in these conditions, Ms. Carlyle. All things considered, I can accept the lack of a decent formal dressing room for the Lead—"

I swallowed a comment.

"—but I must have private space not only to prepare myself but also, now, to safeguard not only my valuables but my costume itself?"

Despite almost losing it at the second "not only" I grabbed for calm as two student handlers and their dogs ran past, giggling and barking, and accepted the shredded, drool-covered cravat. "I can see it's upsetting, Professor. I will try to establish a more secure—Boomer, no!"

Roche turned at my bellow, so instead of being jumped from behind he caught two dinner plate-sized paws to the sternum. With an "oof" he landed square on the seat of his velvet pirate pants, hands up in a useless attempt to fend off the attack.

The shelter had no idea what breed mix Boomer was (current bet was a Newfoundland/Mastodon cross) but at an estimated eleven months old, big as a bathtub, and still growing, he loved everyone. Enthusiastically. Shelter volunteers were trying to work some manners into him to make him more adoptable, but in the meantime, he greeted friends and strangers alike as if they were Ulysses returning from twenty years at sea.

"*Get it off me!*" Roche sputtered from somewhere underneath about 120 pounds of slobbering puppy, so I grabbed Boomer's collar and yanked back as hard as I could. In a flash he transferred his attention to me in an affectionate lean I managed to brace against. Big brown eyes stared up at me adoringly and his tongue lolled out in doggy bliss, slightly marred by the fact he was now wearing Hook's moustache.

Don't laugh don't laugh god please don't laugh. I helped Roche to his feet and brushed at the shag rug's worth of brown fur all over the front of his red velvet pirate coat, but he slapped my hands away. "That is *it!*" he snarled, stooping to snatch Hook's tricorn hat from the ground, slammed it on his head, and stalked off, muttering to himself.

"I got him." Hendrix came trotting up, leash in hand. Part-time football coach and full-time sheriff, he had the size to keep our puppy in line, supplemented by pockets of dog treats. "Sorry, Linds," he said as he clipped the leash onto Boomer's collar. "Big dude broke the tie I had left him at. There's just so much going on that captures his attention."

I sighed. "No worries, Hendrix, though you might be playing Captain Hook if the Professor quits."

There was a warm chuckle behind me. "Oh, Johnathan won't give up the spotlight that easily, my dears. Let me go calm him down. I promise Samuel won't have to learn that Tarantella piece."

Keeping Boomer in close heel to the left, Hendrix grinned down at the tiny woman at his right. "That is truly good news, Mrs. Gantry. No one wants to hear me sing."

"Now, Samuel. You were just fine in choir." Mrs. Gantry was the only one in town who called him "Samuel"; even his mother called the sheriff "Hendrix".

"If luck holds no one will have to hear how long ago eighth grade choir was. I'm going to take this goofball out to my truck and get him a nap, Linds. Let me know when you'd like him back." As by far the biggest and furriest canine available, Boomer had been assigned to play the Darlings' dog, Nana. If only he didn't keep breaking tie-outs.

I waved them off, then turned to my old music and choir teacher with a fond smile.

Though retired after nearly sixty years teaching at Decatur Elementary, Eugenia Gantry still volunteered for every school function and a great deal beyond. Fall concerts, spring plays, decorations for the harvest festival and winter carnival, the summer's Decatur Days celebration . . . Mrs. Gantry was there, driving to and fro in her ancient Plymouth Duster. Her trusty knitting bag came with her, half-finished baby blanket or scarf peeking out as she knitted something to donate toward a local fundraiser.

Between all the volunteer work and time spent puttering in the yard of her small house, I wasn't sure when the woman took a moment off. As the thought occurred, I noticed how tired she looked. I reached out and took her hands between my own.

"Mrs. Gantry, you are truly wonderful. If anyone can talk the professor off the ledge, it's you." There was a sudden crash and a yelp—of the human kind—from the far side of the room where the Lost Boys were practicing, so I squeezed her hands very gently in thanks, then turned to see what the newest crisis was.

MRS. GANTRY WORKED her magic. The Professor overcame his snit thanks to Principal Collins offering her office as a dressing room and—thanks to the hardware store donating pet cleaner and use of a rug shampooer to save the stage during dress rehearsal—there were no other major crises during rehearsals.

Oh, there were the usual minor ones. Our understudy Peter Pan and one of the mermaids got mono. The set crew ran out of brown paint for the "pirate ship" and tried to mix their own, so the starboard side of the *Jolly Roger* was a sort of muddy magenta. A truly unfortunate typo in the program did not quite thank parents who helped with all the skits. One tiny Lost Boy burst into terrified shrieks when she set foot on stage and had to be rescued. Plus, the little poodle mix who played the crocodile was going to be growing out a coat full of green food dye for months.

But the packed audience Friday night made up for everything.

They cheered the cast both human and canine, and laughed at all the right times and none of the wrong ones, even when the backstage director had to pause the action to clean up a few puddles onstage. They clapped up a storm when Peter begged them to prove they *did* believe in fairies, and when the cat laser toy playing Tinkerbell came back to life, it brought the house down.

When the final curtain lifted for the end call, the spotlight found Mrs. Gantry at her piano. As the audience roared for her just as it had for sixty-odd years, I had to wipe away a tear.

Then the curtain dropped and we. Were. Done.

Next to me, Roche was blowing his nose on the lace of his sleeve. He caught my eye, cleared his throat hurriedly, and smiled. "Well, Ms. Carlyle, I would consider this a success."

I smiled back. "You bet, Professor. The kids all had a great time, everyone loved your Captain Hook, and we just raised a lot of money for the shelter."

"Yes, well." He coughed. "I must admit, that Border Collie who played Smee was surprisingly talented. I felt a real connection during our scenes. I may go down there Monday morning and see if there is anything beyond the spark of the performance, so to speak."

My smile widened. "I think that's a great idea."

CLOSING DOWN A play can be almost as much work as setting one up. Even with sending students home in their costumes, there were dozens of coats to sort through, and rain had added assorted umbrellas, rain boots, and hats to the pile. Though I would lock everything up when I left, the sound crew still had to secure microphone pickups and power down the ancient mixing board. The lighting crew had a long check-down list to make sure everything was off. Most of the set pieces from the nursery, including the bedding, rocking chair, lamps, and still-damp area rugs were borrowed and had to be tagged for return to their owners on Sunday.

We were down to only a handful of people when Hendrix approached. "Linds, we need to talk. Principal Collins just told me the till is empty."

His words did not make sense. "What till?"

"The till, the box office, whatever you theatre people call it. All the money is missing."

"*What?*" Everyone left backstage turned to look at me and I struggled to lower my voice. "What do you mean, all the money is missing?"

Hendrix shrugged, looking grim. "Collins thought she had locked her office up, but the door was open when she went to get her coat, and the cash box is empty."

Our auditorium could seat over four hundred people and we had charged ten dollars per ticket. "That's four thousand dollars, Hendrix!" I lowered my voice further. "You don't think the Professor . . . ?"

"It could be anyone with a key or other access to that office. Speaking of which," he looked around casually, "any chance you could open your purse for me real quick?"

It took me a second, then I felt myself flush. "Are you *kidding* me!"

He had the decency to look embarrassed. "Listen, Linds, I need to do this proper. Otherwise there's going to be gossip. You know that."

"Fine." I stalked over to where my coat and purse lay, grabbed them, and handed them over. "Search away. Going to pat me down, too?"

Hendrix looked up from squeezing my coat pockets and grinned. "Not unless you go to prom with me again."

"Dammit, Hendrix!"

He handed my coat back, opened and briefly looked into my purse, handed that to me as well. "I get it, Linds. But with you clear, we can concentrate on figuring out how to approach Captain Hook over there," he nodded stage left, where Collins, Mrs. Gantry, and Roche stood chatting. "I asked her to delay him just a bit."

I eyed the Professor's tight velvet pirate pants. "How big a stack of money is four thousand dollars?"

He cocked his head to the side, looked over at Roche, coatless in his white poofy pirate shirt, and nodded. "I get what you mean. He won't have it on him, not in those pants. Won't fit in his boots, either. It's likely with his street clothes, especially if he brought a duffel bag with him."

"Don't you need a warrant to search his bag?"

Hendrix sighed. "Not for this—probable cause and all. But if he raises a big enough stink, everyone will know, and Collins asked me to try to be discreet." He squared his shoulders and took a deep breath.

Which turned into a "No! Boomer, *sit!*" as the puppy bounded into view from the wings, saw three humans just standing there when they could be petting him, and barrelled joyously into the group. Roche hit the deck again, but Principal Collins managed to keep Mrs. Gantry upright, though her knitting bag went flying. For once Boomer didn't press his advantage but in a surprisingly controlled move, simply leaned against Mrs. Gantry to gaze up at her adoringly.

"Well, aren't you just a big sweetie?" Mrs. Gantry reached out to scratch behind a furry ear. Boomer's tail thumped madly and he leaned harder, but Collins was still bracing the elderly women from the other side so there was only minor staggering.

"Going to add 'dog charmer' to your volunteering?" I asked her, giving the grumbling professor a hand up.

"'Menace control' is more like it," Roche huffed.

"Before all that, perhaps you can explain this first, Mrs. Gantry?" Hendrix held up the knitting bag, money peeking out of it like odd green yarn.

In the stunned silence, Boomer put his nose under Mrs. Gantry's hand and nudged but she ignored him, looking Hendrix in the eye. "No, Samuel, I do not believe I can."

"But—why?" I was already exhausted and this tipped me almost into tears. "I don't understand. Why would you do this? You always help! For everything!"

"And no one ever helps me!" Mrs. Gantry's eyes were suddenly full. "All these years I dedicated my life to this school and this town and it's like I'm forgotten until someone needs something from me. I was a music teacher all those years: I can't afford to hire someone to mow my lawn or repair my car, winter heating season is coming, and on top of it all, I need a new roof. I would have paid it back somehow, but now? I don't know how I'll get through another winter." She started to cry, quiet sobs that ripped into my chest.

A muscle twitched in Hendrix's jaw but he squared his shoulders again. "Mrs. Gantry, I am truly sorry, but you're going to have to come down to the station with me." He reached out the hand not holding the knitting bag to take her by the arm.

The sudden rumbling vibrated through the soles of my shoes, and for a moment I thought someone had started up the ancient backstage generator that used to power the stage lights.

It was deep and it was menacing.

Boomer was growling.

Hendrix froze, looking at the huge puppy sitting on Mrs. Gantry's foot. "Boomer, be a good boy," he said calmly, but Boomer only pressed closer against her shins. He looked Hendrix dead in the eye, lifted a lip, and growled louder.

Hendrix lowered his hand and took a very careful step back. Everyone held their breath, then Boomer looked up at Mrs. Gantry and wagged his tail.

"The furry menace may have a point," said Roche, and Principal Collins nodded. "I think we have a better idea."

THE CROWD WAS possibly even more enthusiastic the second time around. "Back by Popular Demand" read the flyers. "For One More Night Only!" The house was just as packed and the funds raised were even higher. Mrs. Gantry got her roof plus an energy efficient new furnace. The local scout troop took on mowing, raking, and shovelling duties, and Hendrix got nice and greasy tackling some much-needed maintenance on that ancient Plymouth. Principal Collins and the professor set up an online video tutorial program for beginning piano students, and former Decatur kids all around the country signed their children up for lessons.

Despite the influx of new students, Mrs. Gantry stopped looking so tired all the time, and when the local craft store began donating yarn, her knitting output increased exponentially.

"BUT I DON'T want to be an orphan!"

I stifled a sigh. "Orphans are important, Jocelyn. It's right in the name. You can't do Little Orphan Annie without having orphans."

"I don't care." She stuck her lip out. "Why can't I play Annie?"

"Because it's a hard knock life, Sweetie. Now, go practice and remember," I patted her shoulder, "you're July, the *silent* orphan. You will have to be very expressive in your acting. That's why you get special billing."

She flounced away, satisfied, as I straightened and stretched my back. Our set was coming along nicely. The PVC pipes Hendrix had painted grey and assembled into bed frames came out better than I had hoped, with yards of old fabric from the local craft store making up pretty good orphan beds. The muddy magenta boards recycled from the *Jolly Roger* made grim-looking walls. All in all, this was one awesomely depressing orphanage.

I looked around the stage. Professor Roche was reading lines to himself as Daddy Warbucks; Liza, his border collie, listening so carefully I half-expected her to start reading back.

"Quack!"

I jumped at the voice in my ear. "Dammit, Hendrix! Knock it off. FDR doesn't 'quack'!"

He chuckled around the black plastic cigarette holder clenched in his teeth. "Can I help it if this makes me feel more like the Penguin than the President?"

"Yes. Yes, you can. Now, go get Boomer—it's time to work on his scenes with Annie."

Still chuckling, Hendrix pulled the leash out of his pocket and headed toward the practice room, where Mrs. Gantry was hammering out "Little Girls" as the senior playing Miss Hannigan practiced. Boomer would be there, chin on his front paws and ears twitching. He hadn't left Mrs. Gantry's side since that night last fall, and had mellowed considerably under her tutelage; apparently, after sixty years of teaching schoolchildren, training one oversized puppy was not a problem.

Good thing, as the "Mastodon" guess was looking more and more likely . . . at 150 pounds and still growing, Boomer could now carry Mrs. Gantry to safety if she ever slipped and fell on one of their quiet nighttime walks. In the meantime, he was Sandy for our spring play and kept Mrs. Gantry's feet warm when she wasn't working the pedals on her piano.

I took one more look around, mentally cataloguing what props and materials could be used for one more play to support our shoestring budget. I had already decided on *The Wizard of Oz* for next Fall.

Boomer was going to make one truly spectacular Toto.

WHAT GOLD SMELLS LIKE

FRANCES PAULI

THE GREATEST BLOODHOUND in all of history teetered on the edge of a ragged plank. Below her, the sea thrashed an angry dance. At her back, the stupidest crew of pirates she'd ever encountered howled and prodded her with their rusty swords. Considering her current predicament, she had to wonder what that said about her.

"Get movin'," a buck-toothed poodle shouted and stamped his peg leg.

"Jump!" The chorus washed through the crew like a tidal wave.

In the centre of the idiots, their king stood, arms crossed and plumed hat fluttering as if it meant to sprout real wings and fly off his vacant head. He was a collie, one of those yappy black-and-white breeds that she'd found were often all bark and no action. Except today. Today, he'd picked a rotten time to get serious.

"Give her the heave," he commanded. "And put her out of my misery."

"You don't want to do that," The Nose called back to him, giving the sea a nervous eye and curling her claws against the splintery wood. "I'm worth more to you alive than feeding the fishes."

"Scat," the captain cursed. "Ain't no she-dog ever been more than a curse on a ship."

"Crew of the *Widowmaker* didn't think so, Sir," she declared.

"So you say," the collie stated in a too-merry voice. "But we found you abandoned on her decks, did we not? Were she a ghost ship? Did you feed 'em all to the fishies before I sunk you?"

His crew, as if on reflex, turned to the railing and the thrashing sea. There, just off the port side, the remnants of the bloodhound's former vessel could still be spied. Bits of board and barrels, a wash of detritus shifting atop the waves marked, at least for the moment, the *Widow*'s resting place.

The sight of the wreckage put a growl in The Nose's belly. It rose like a cobra all the way to the back of her throat. Her lip curled, and she took a half step back toward the deck of the *Shrike*.

"No you don't." The collie captain waved his sabre in her direction. "Into the brine with you."

The Nose swallowed her rage and remembered that she had a neck to save. Her head hung, and she shook herself sadly, throwing a cloud of loose hair and a few fleas into the salt air.

"It's your loss." She put a plaintive note behind the words. "But he's a fool that tosses a gold detector overboard without so much as a test of it."

She took a long step back to the end of the plank, threw one paw out to hover above empty air. Below, the waves licked hungrily at the ship's sides.

"Wait." It took the pirate captain two breaths longer than she'd have liked to stop her. "What's this about a gold detector?" he asked.

The Nose turned over her shoulder. She teetered dramatically and then set both paws firmly back against the board. "Me," she said. "I can smell a gold doubloon a league away."

"Scat," the captain barked. "No one can smell that far."

"I can," the bloodhound stood proudly, puffed out her chest, and gave him a squint-eyed appraisal. "If I feel like it."

"Prove it," the collie said. "Prove it or swim."

"You've got four doubloons in your left coat pocket," the bloodhound said. She sniffed the air dramatically. "Three Spanish and one you plucked from the *Widow*'s coffers."

"Just for luck," he said. "But you're wrong."

"I'm never wrong," she said.

"Get ready to dive." The collie fished one paw into his pocket. "I have five . . ."

"Four," The Nose said.

The collie frowned.

"But that fellow behind you has one in *his* pocket," the bloodhound announced.

The peg-legged poodle whimpered.

His captain spun around, and the sabre flashed, reflecting the sun's light just as the waves had. Its point aimed straight at the curl-covered poodle, and he growled a warning, a low rumble before demanding, "Turn out your pockets."

"I-it fell out o' yer coat," the poodle began. "I only grabbed it to give back—"

The sword moved too fast. Faster than the bloodhound expected. She'd have to remember that—the quick blade, the short temper. Its point hovered at the poodle's throat, and two of the nearby pirates shuffled forward to grab the duplicitous dog by both arms. The missing coin was quickly retrieved from the poodle's pockets, and the captain took it with a snarl.

"Take him to the brig," he ordered.

The crew wasted no time obeying, and as the poodle's crewmates dragged him away, The Nose took a confident step back down the plank.

"Wait." The collie captain's voice brooked no argument.

The Nose froze. She cast a nervous eye around the crew, caught sight of a bedraggled, half-starved Shih Tzu at the back of the mob. He winked at her.

"What does it smell like?" the collie asked.

"Sir?" the bloodhound dragged her gaze back to the captain.

"Gold," he snapped. "What does it smell like?"

It was an easy question. Everyone knew what gold smelled like. The bloodhound let her gaze drift out to sea, to the place where the *Widowmaker* had gone down. She swallowed hard. "Blood," she said.

"Remember that," the captain said. "Just you keep that firmly in your mind."

She nodded. It meant she'd won, of course. He'd keep her on board for now, keep her out of the briny sea. But, as the crew returned to their duties, she knew she'd only borrowed time. She still had a neck to save.

Her eyes drifted to the poor Shih Tzu.

Maybe two.

"What do they call you?" the captain asked.

He was known as Horace Hellbound, and he'd sunk her ship. His cannons had torn the *Widowmaker* to shreds, and she wouldn't forget that any more than she'd forget how fast his blade was. His reputation sailed the seas ahead of him, a tale of short fuses and long memory. They said he could smell a lie a mile away.

The bloodhound smiled at him.

"They called me The Nose," she said.

EVERYONE KNEW THAT gold smelled like blood. That was true. The Nose knew, however, that it also smelled like every paw that had ever touched it. Each doubloon on the captain's table had a history, a story that snaked back through dozens of greedy dogs.

The room around her suggested its owner was just another of the same. The bedclothes were silken, the candlesticks studded with gems. There were chests in every corner, shining lamps, shimmering jewels, and a library that rivalled the one she'd enjoyed on the *Widowmaker*.

Just thinking of that loss put the growl back in her voice, however, and she quickly swallowed the memory.

"What about this one." Horace Hellbound thrust another shiny coin in her direction.

The Nose held it to her nostrils. An empty gesture. She could smell it all without trying. The odours clinging to the pirate's treasure hung in the air around it, a library in their own right, telling tales.

"This one you earned," she said.

"I never did!" He flinched but snatched the coin from her paw and tucked it quickly into his vest pocket. "Try another one."

"An honest day's work?" she asked.

"Leave it," he said, waving a paw at her and scampering around the table. He'd piled so much gold there that it dribbled from the edges, puddling on the floor, and making the carpet shine. "This one. Tell me about this cup."

She took the vessel he shoved in her direction and made a show of smelling it, closing her eyes and sighing softly. The dog was the sort of captain to flaunt his rank, to wear a feathered hat that would mark his status all the way across the sea. It would make him an easy target, and though some might call that bravery, The Nose labelled him a fool.

Once the crew had been shut out and the door latched, however, he bounced around the table like a pup, shuffling through his hoard. His tail never stopped wagging.

"This is interesting," she lied. "But it's not gold."

"Ahh." The collie nodded fiercely. "I knew it was painted."

"Oh, it's not painted," The Nose said. "It's plated, just a thin layer of the real stuff over lead."

"Counterfeit." His tail paused long enough for a growl to squeeze out. "Those bastards."

The Nose leaned back in her chair and set the chintzy cup down amid the captain's gold. She watched him, and she kept her expression in tight control. He'd been testing her for most of the afternoon, and she could see the sun sinking toward the waves through his ornate, coloured glass windows.

The ship rocked gently now that the chaos of battle had ended, but The Nose settled in on the new vessel fully aware of how precarious her position was.

"One more," the collie said. He left the table, crossed the room, and with his back to her, rummaged in one of the smaller chests. When he turned back around, a chain dangled from his paws. He returned to the table and laid an ornate pocket watch in front of her. "Tell me about this."

The Nose inhaled. Her saggy jowls shivered as she turned her head left and right above the watch. This treasure was more than plated. The gold had the metallic, bloody odour, true and thick. Behind that, she could smell the pirate captain. The collie's personal scent wrapped his watch in a cloud of ownership.

"You've had this a long time," she said.

"Anyone could have guessed that."

"All your life," The Nose continued. She was a bloodhound through and through, but she was also a diplomat. She'd learned over the years not to simply blurt out what you smelled without exercising some caution. "It was a gift."

"Now, how could you smell that?" The collie frowned at her, lowering his ears and dropping his tail. But he didn't deny it.

Behind his signature odour, The Nose smelled a different sort of dog, a mean dog. The watch's last owner had been vicious to the point of cruelty. He also smelled a great deal like his son, and so she bit her tongue and gave the safest answer possible.

"Your father."

"A great dog," the collie answered. He also cringed, shivered, and let his muzzle fall toward his toes. "You definitely have a skill," he said. "Which will be of use to me. So long as that remains true, you can remain on the *Shrike*. As soon as it is no longer true, you shall not remain anywhere."

"Of course." The Nose tilted her head in a gesture of agreement, a submissive gesture that put a burr in her backside.

Necessary.

"You may go," the collie said. "Find your bed among the crew, the galley if yer belly needs it, and some useful work until we make landfall."

"Where do we sail?" She perked slightly, inhaled, and smelled his mistrust of her.

"None of yer business." He took a step around the table, sweeping a clatter of gold to the carpet with his wagging tail.

The Nose nodded and turned her back on him. She reached for the door, pausing when he spoke once again.

"What did he smell like?" The collie's voice was low and level, backed by the softest trace of a growl. "My father? What was it?"

"Violence." She gave him a simple answer.

"And me?"

Here she had to tread even more lightly. If this pirate could smell a lie, The Nose would have to give him some version of the truth. She inhaled, used the gesture to buy a moment, to think fast.

"You smell like danger," she said.

The collie took a long breath to answer, paused enough to make her sweat. Had she played to his ego, or played her own cards too soon?

"Remember that," he said. "Danger."

"Of course, captain." The bloodhound dipped her head. She opened the cabin door and slipped free, intact, in place, and definitely in danger.

THE SHIP'S GALLEY lay in her ample belly. The crew collected at a disorderly chaos of rickety tables, and in one corner, a fat iron pot was manned by the ship's cook. From its sloppy rim, the scent of boiled cabbage and dead fish wafted in an unpleasant cloud. The cook, a stringy-coated sheepdog as round as his pot, stirred this foul concoction, ladling out bowl after bowl as the pirates circled the room.

The Nose found the end of the line, snagged a wooden bowl from a stack near the door, and tried not to breathe too deeply.

As she waited for her turn, The Nose spotted the scruffy-looking Shih Tzu. He'd already fetched himself a bowl of chow and stood at the far end of the tables, looking for a place to sit. While she watched, a pair of terriers approached the smaller dog.

The terriers swaggered toward the wretched dog, and their ears were flat and slick against their heads. Two wire-haired tails stuck out behind them, still and wag-less. The Nose knew it wasn't going to be good but she needed to stay out of it, needed to not draw attention to herself.

She eased forward as the line moved, but she kept her eyes fixed on the drama as it played out.

The Shih Tzu cringed and clung to his wooden bowl. He slunk around the nearest table, but his path was blocked by a sea of legs. The pirates sitting there suddenly felt the desire to stretch, blocking the aisle between them.

The Nose dropped her tail and inhaled the scent of conspiracy. She felt a growl rising.

The Shih Tzu backed up, hugging the wall and searching for an alternate route, but the terriers had already managed to corner him. They closed in, and the Nose sank her claws into her wooden bowl to keep from snarling.

From the corner there came a high-pitched yipping. Something clattered and splashed. The terriers moved aside, snickering, passing the spot and walking into a magically clear aisle to find their seats. In their wake, the Shih Tzu crouched over his spilled supper. His paws reached for what he could scrape from the filthy floor, tucking and scooping as much food back into the bowl as possible.

Foul behaviour for a crew, picking on its weakest member. That sort of bullying was never tolerated on the *Widowmaker*. The Nose thought of a ship's crew as a family. She believed it *should* act like one.

"Hey!"

A sharply barked syllable dragged her attention back to the

line. It had moved on without her, and the sheepdog glared at her across his pot. The Nose shook herself and hurried her steps. She thrust out her bowl, and when the cook ladled a measure of fishy broth into it, she stared directly into his eyes. Her ears lifted and swung forward, hackles prickled into a line between her shoulder blades.

The cook stared back, but he was more fluff than substance. Soft around more than his middle. Eventually, he dipped his weapon once more, pulled up another scoop of stew, and doubled her portion.

The Nose lowered her hackles and drifted out of line. A submissive cook and a pair of bullies. A crew that cared more about sport than each other. That stole from their captain. She'd landed in the worst possible place, and she had no time to waste on any of them.

She stretched her neck, stood taller, and strode with her overflowing bowl directly to the Shih Tzu. It would cause waves, might even give her away too soon, but she'd had about all she could take for one day. When The Nose reached the little dog, cowering against a wall and lapping at his soiled food, she didn't hesitate. She bent down, tipped her bowl into his near-empty one, and gazed for a half-second into his watery, tear-stained brown eyes.

The Nose winked and the Shih Tzu wagged his tail, brushing a clean arc against the dirty wall. She stood quickly, but leaned against the wall beside him, and ate slowly. She took her time, and she made sure the smaller dog had had his fill before she left him.

"MORE TESTS?" THE Nose awoke to the captain's barking. He stood over her, paws on his hips, and when she sat up, threw a thin blindfold at her.

"Put that on."

The bloodhound groaned and scratched behind one ear. She'd fallen asleep on deck, wedged up against the railing and away from the rest of the crew, who slept in a pile that would have scared away any sane dog. She itched just thinking about the fleas, the drool, and the ringworm she'd spotted on the bulldog first mate's left hindquarter.

"What's it for?" she asked, buying time, scrambling for a plan in case he meant to toss her overboard today.

"Testing," he announced. "You claimed you could smell gold at a great distance."

"No claim about it," The Nose said, relaxing a bit. "I can and I do."

"You do?"

"We're heading for it," she said. "Been on a collision course for over a day now, I reckon."

"Get up." The collie tried to sound intimidating, but his silly tail moved nonstop behind him. He was excited, and she didn't have to smell the treasure he sought to see it had him in its grip. "Put that on."

"Fine." She staggered to her feet, hips complaining about the night on hard wooden planks. "I'll put it on, but it won't do any good. My nose sees better than the old eyes anyway."

She plucked up the blindfold and began to wrap it around her head.

"I hear you made friends with the Goob," the captain said merrily. "Not a very wise move among this lot."

"Little dogs have their place," she said, fashioning a knot at the back of her head. "And their purpose. No one deserves to be kicked about like that."

"Goob's no one," the captain shrugged. "And the crew needs their sport. Keeps them mellow on the long hauls."

The Nose believed keeping the crew in line was the captain's job, but she said nothing. She'd tied the cloth tightly around her head and could see nothing through it. The collie's fur smelled like pipe smoke and whiskey, however, and she had no trouble following him across the deck to the overpowering odour of his assembled crew.

They'd clustered together, and the smell of their combined musk brought tears to her veiled eyes.

"Stand aside, now," the captain ordered. "Give her room."

The tide of odour parted, and in its centre, The Nose sensed the open deck. She feared again that this was her ticket overboard. Then the sea air brought her a new string of scents. She relaxed and waited.

"Before you stand three chests," Horace Hellbound announced. "Each is full to its brim with cool, wet-packed sand. In the centre of one, a single doubloon waits."

"The left one," The Nose said, throwing out a paw to point directly at the gold. "Just there."

"She didn't let him finish," a rough voice grumbled to her right.

It was followed by the roar of a dissatisfied crew. They'd come for a show, and she'd robbed them of that pleasure.

Serves them all right.

"Shut up!" the captain yapped.

"She done cheated," someone whined.

"You can take that off now," Horace spoke to her softly, then barked at his crew in a series of screeching, unintelligible bursts.

The Nose slid the blindfold free and eyed the chests impassively.

"You lot." The collie aimed a paw at the two terriers who had hassled Goob. "You filled these below deck?"

"We did," the taller terrier said sulkily. "An' Drake done watched over her while she was sleeping. No way she could've sneaked up on us."

Beside them, the wormy bulldog scratched at his hind end. When one of the terriers jabbed him, he snapped to attention. "She din' so much as twitch," he said.

"And the Goob?" the collie asked.

"In the clink since yesterday, locked up tight just like you says."

"Very well." Horace stuffed his feathered hat down low over his ears and faced The Nose. "You've proven yourself to my thinking," he said. "Tomorrow we make land, and we'll see what that sniffer of yours can do for us."

The Nose nodded. She'd passed his tests. Any fool could see the gold lust shining in his eyes. She'd earned her place on his next treasure hunt, but something more significant bothered her now. Goob was locked up. Incarcerated. No doubt on account of her.

And that just wouldn't do at all.

"So you took this map off a prisoner, but it shows three different Xs," The Nose reclined in the captain's cabin, legs up so that she could rest her rear paws atop his treasure. She held the chintzy, gold-plated cup, and waved it so wildly that the rum inside sloshed on his carpet. "And you don't know which one has the gold."

"Yes."

"Why not just dig all three?" she asked.

"Traps," Horace said. His words already slurred, and he barely lifted his head from where he'd lain it atop the table. He sat opposite her and had drunk far more. "This particular captain is known for their deadly decoys. Even so, that *was* the plan before we found you."

The Nose quickly hid a prideful smirk.

"I've heard of this, Skullbones Atoll," she said. "The whole spit is supposed to be riddled with booby-traps."

"Rumours," the captain mumbled. He drifted for a moment, head bobbing back toward the table. Then he jerked upright. "But you fixed that, too."

"I did?" The Nose frowned and blew out so that her jowls danced.

"Gave me the idea," Horace said. "All dogs have their uses, you said. Gonna send the Goob in first to spring 'em."

"And if he gets killed in the process?" The Nose watched the collie closely. More than that, she smelled him. He reeked of booze, and fleas, and not a hint of regret.

He shrugged, laid his head back atop the table, and began to chuckle.

The bloodhound smelled him, and she spun her plans around his fool neck like a noose.

THEY SPIED THE atoll at first light. By high noon they'd dropped anchor, and Horace Hellbound's crew piled into the twin yawls and began to row for shore. The collie left no one on board, either too cocky to fear an attack from behind, or too insecure to trust any of his pirates not to pull anchor and ditch him on the atoll.

He was a poor captain, and The Nose watched him from the prow of the second yawl with a growing dislike roiling in her stomach. He perched in the nose of the other rowboat, and he'd shackled Goob to the gunwale for no good reason except to show her that he could.

The little Shih Tzu shivered and hunkered lower in the boat.

By the time they made land, her fur had soaked up so much salt air that it dragged at her bones. All the pirates climbed from the yawls with heavy treads, staggering onto the beach or simply folding into a sit right at the edge of the waves. Even the captain sprang from his perch with less of his usual swagger. The others unhooked Goob, and the huge shaggy chef all but tossed the smaller dog onto the sands.

"We've no time to rest," Horace shouted, making a show of eyeballing the spit where they'd landed. "Swallow yer tongues and get ready to move out."

The atoll lay bare and narrow here. It curved like a crescent moon in either direction, and they'd come to shore in the middle. To the left, long grasses broke through the sand and the far point turned rocky and jagged. To the right, a stubby forest covered the strip of land, growing in a green band between the unending sea and the brilliant, still lagoon at the atoll's centre.

Horace Hellbound stood on the beach with his ears up and his tail swinging. He squinted toward the trees and the rocks in turn, and then he aimed his gaze inward at the jewel of the lagoon.

"Bring the Goob!" he shouted. "We'll cross inland."

"You'd dig the easy hole first." The Nose padded toward the collie. "I suppose that's a safe choice."

"Safe has nothing to do with it," the collie snapped. "Just happens to be the best landing."

She nodded and followed his gaze toward the lagoon. Goob limped up beside the collie, looking even more bedraggled than usual and dragging the chain they'd left hanging from a ring around his neck. He sniffled, and The Nose bared her teeth.

"Onward," the captain ordered. "Lead the way, Goob. Twenty paces to the water and a sharp ten more in the direction of the stones."

The Shih Tzu started off, gingerly at first and then rising into a confident trot. After went the collie captain, and The Nose positioned herself directly behind him. She gave the crew her back, but she heard them, grumbling and groaning, losing ground as the pace increased.

They trod across the sandy spit, over the hump at the middle of the crescent and down a gentle slope to the rim of the lagoon. There, Goob turned obediently toward the distant rocks. He continued for ten more paces, then sat on his haunches while the rest caught up with him.

The captain withdrew his map, which had been folded roughly and stuffed into the inside of his jacket. He frowned at it, then waved one paw toward Goob.

"Run in a bit of a circle here," he said.

The Nose growled.

The little dog obeyed, however, scampering in a series of off-round circuits until the collie finally ordered him to stop.

The pirate, assured of his safety, turned to The Nose. "What do you smell?" he asked.

The Nose relaxed. This would be the tricky bit, for she'd come to believe that Horace could, in fact, smell a lie. She'd have to select her words quite carefully, and she took a long moment to sniff the air while her thoughts churned.

"I smell sand and sea," she said. "Salt air and a crew of mangy pirates."

"Do you smell gold?" he demanded.

"Yes," The Nose said, adding quickly, "you have five doubloons in your pocket."

"Chew the doubloons," the collie cursed. "Do you smell gold there, under the sand?"

She did, but she'd no intention of telling him that. The Nose got down on all fours, pressed her snout to the sand, and wracked her brain for an answer that would not be a lie.

"Well?" the captain squatted beside her. "Do you smell it? Is my gold here?"

Eureka. The bloodhound woofed, riffling her jowls, and shook her head. "I do not smell your gold," she said.

After all, the treasure would belong to whoever dug it up, and she meant to deprive this pirate of that luxury. She would not allow him to take anything else that was hers.

Horace howled and stamped one paw against the sand. He stood, whipping her with his flag tail as he spun to face the crew again. "About face, everyone," he shouted. "We'll move on to the trees before—"

His order was cut off by the squeals of a dog in pain and terror. The sound pressed The Nose lower to the sands, made her clap her paws over her long ears and whine. It went on far too long yet was cut short so abruptly that a chill wandered up her spine.

"Look there!" one of the pirates shouted. A paw flew out, followed by another and another. All eyes turned to the lagoon and a cloud of crimson staining the clear blue surface. The pirates yipped and huddled closer together, farther from the shore. Even

Horace backed apace alongside them.

The Nose stood and glared into the lagoon. She squinted at the shimmering water, at the blood and the deep, sandy bottom. She knew exactly what had happened, but it took the crew a long breath more to come to a deduction of their own.

Then, they whispered a name between them. Passed it back and forth, from muzzle to muzzle, until the captain finally barked them to silence. A grim shroud fell over the company, and as they marched away from the lagoon, more than one head turned to gaze back, to stare toward the last spot where they'd seen the Goob.

A stretch of sand which was now, pointedly, vacant.

THEY WERE SLOWER going once inside the trees, as if each segment of the atoll had its own way of eating at them. The crew dragged and continued to grumble, and the way grew choked with thorns that jabbed at paw pads and snagged in the fur.

The Nose sulked at the back of the pack, picking her way to avoid as many scratches as possible. She dragged at the tail of the crew, and she listened to them whispering of the Goob's demise. Now, when the little dog was gone, they were sorry.

She curled her lip and let her jowls froth. Her tail slung behind her like a sabre, and she followed the pirates with their crimes lining up before her in testimony. They deserved whatever they got, this crew. And she would not be sorry to see them pay.

The atoll turned chilly as the trees blotted out the sun. It might only have been her mood. By the time the captain called her forward, her fur bristled. The Nose shook herself, woofed softly, and jogged through the aisle they made to the place where Horace Hellbound perched atop a short stump.

"There you are," he said. "Thought you'd run off on us."

"Where would I go?" The Nose asked.

"Indeed." The collie's blade danced free of its sheath, singing a song of steel beneath the trees. He wagged his tail and pointed with the sword toward a break in the foliage. "In you go," he said.

So, she would be his trap tester now.

The Nose huffed, shook her jowls loose, and eyed the dark trail. She might have argued that she was too valuable to risk, but there was no need. There was no gold buried on this stretch of the atoll, and she knew where all the traps lay.

With an exaggerated shrug, she bent low and tucked herself into the brambles. The captain followed on her heel, came breathing like an overheated Saint Bernard. His lust was thick on him, and that would make the next step so much easier.

She led him through the tangle of brush, out the other side, and six paces past the place marked upon his map. When he called her back, The Nose did her best to look surprised.

"Back here." The collie stood far too close to the target. "Don't you smell it?"

The Nose took a huge breath. She turned her head away from the Captain, took a long step to the side to lead him. She sniffed loud and long, and the pirate stepped away from the trap. The Nose exhaled and shook her head.

"I don't smell nothing," she said.

"Then you do smell something?" Horace frowned, ears drooping, tail hanging limp behind him.

"No gold," The Nose said. She stepped back, flanked him, and moved into his shadow. "I guess it's not h—"

She let the word morph into a howl as she triggered the trap. Her rear paw kicked at a seemingly random stone, and the sandy ground beneath her fell away. The Nose dropped into the pit, and she remembered to yip like an injured Shih Tzu when she hit bottom.

Far above, Horace Hellbound cursed and shouted for his crew.

At the bottom of the trap, The Nose scratched her claws through the sand until water began to seep into the pit.

"Help!" she cried. "Tide's coming in."

"Woo hoo!" Hellbound's shaggy face appeared in the circle of light above. "What a mess you've gotten yourself into."

"I can't climb up," The Nose called to him. "Can you lower a rope?"

She held her breath. Everything depended on his next move.

"I could," the pirate captain drawled. "Sure, I could. We have some rope. Yes."

The Nose watched him, inhaling the bitter aroma of deception.

"I think," the collie continued. "That you have been very useful. But with two sites eliminated, I know exactly where to dig."

"You're a bastard," The Nose shouted. "Just like your old

man."

She couldn't see much from her position, only his face and a halo of pale green forest. She was still sure he cringed at the mention of his sire.

"Maybe I am," he yelled down. "But *you* are no longer necessary."

He moved aside, and she was left to stare up at the sun-dappled leaves. Hellbound shouted orders, a muffled yapping sound, and the pirates crashed away through the trees. They'd head for the rocks now, for the far end of the atoll, the hardest spot to dig.

It would take them days to work out they'd been had.

The Nose listened to their departure while the water rose. By the time she turned away from the sun, it lapped warm and salty against her knees. She could touch all sides of the pit with her arms outstretched, and she probed and felt her way through a full circuit. The water reached her waist by the time she finally found the lever.

The Nose grinned. She craned her head back, smiled at the sun and the trees and fading sound of pirate voices. Then she took a deep breath and ducked under the water.

WHERE THE NOSE swam free of the tunnel, the lagoon was sapphire blue and still as a mirror. Until she broke the surface, that is, sputtering and cursing the years that had made her lungs less capable. Her chest ached, and she floated a moment on her back to catch her breath before paddling for shore.

There, she dragged her soggy carcass up onto the dry sand and sprawled there, alive, wet, and with all her associated bits intact.

She let the aches in her bones settle, and she listened for any trace of Hellbound's pirates on their way to steal her gold. They'd long moved past this spot, however, and all she heard was the soft kiss of sea against sand from the other side of the spit.

The lagoon made no such comment, and from where she lay, she could see nearly all the way across it. There, the rocky tips met with only a narrow thread of space between them. The Nose sat up and inhaled the scent of freedom.

Pirates were creatures of habit. Stupid pirates were downright predictable. Hellbound's crew would sally forth to the rocks and begin to dig. They'd manage no more than clearing a few stones aside before dusk fell and they had to make camp.

The Nose scrambled to her paws and headed after them. She'd follow only halfway, and she'd keep to the interior shore. While the collie wasted his crew digging rocks, she'd retrieve *her* gold, steal his ship, and be gone again before the sun came up.

Her paws moved quickly once she'd set her mind to the goal. Too quickly. Her own lust would have her kicking at Hellbound's heels if she didn't rein it in. She breathed deep, paused to sniff, and let the pirates take a longer lead. Then she started off again, trotting up the sandy beach which curved softly into a pristine crescent.

The trees to the seaward side faded soon enough. The brambles fell away as the land narrowed, and The Nose went slow and low, hunching forward and moving on silent paws in case the pirates had lingered along the way.

The wind blew in from the sea, which meant it carried her scent out over the lagoon. It also kept her from catching any clues of how far the collie's crew had made it.

The Nose crept forward, ears attuned and nose on alert. She reached the centre stretch of sand, and she retraced the path they'd taken that morning, stepping in the prints made by herself, the captain, and poor Goob. She found the tracks easily enough, and she followed them to the place where the scent of her gold should have wafted thick as blood pudding.

Instead, The Nose smelled only sand and salt. She found only an empty hole, a huge pile of sand, and a series of pawprints crisscrossing themselves around the scene of the crime. The bloodhound stared into a shallower pit this time and marked the square outline in the sand at its bottom.

The place where her treasure had rested.

The place where she'd buried it ten years prior.

She lifted her nose to scent for any trace of the one who'd dug it up, but before she could sniff, a familiar voice spoke from directly behind her.

"Just as we was about to hit them rocks," Horace Hellbound said. "Something told me I should turn right around."

"Did it?" The Nose turned slowly, with her paws spread to the sides in a gesture of peace. She was glad for the caution immediately. For Hellbound had his blade out, and the wicked tip aimed straight for her heart. "Fancy that," she said.

"Fancy that." The collie stepped forward, forcing The Nose backwards.

They moved like a four-legged crab, working their way around the hole until Hellbound could lean to one side and peer down. When he did, The Nose considered lunging for his weapon, but the pirate was fast. She remembered that. He was lightning fast with the sword and more than ready to run her through.

"Stealing my treasure, I see," he said.

"It's not really yours," she replied. "Is it?"

"I'm going to enjoy spilling your guts," Hellbound snarled. His sword tip twitched, and the low sun glinted off the blade. He was the sort of dog who would bite too quickly. The sort of captain who could smell a lie, but who would never think to check for someone sneaking up behind him.

"Where are your men?" The Nose stalled him.

"Digging for gold you already nicked," the pirate snarled. "What did it smell like? When you stole my treasure?"

"It smelled like betrayal." The Nose grinned and braced herself.

She stared into the collie's eyes and saw death staring back at her. His ears were up, and his damn tail hadn't stopped wagging once. She made fists with her paws, flexed her knees, and let a growl loose that started low in her belly.

Hellbound's eyes stretched wide. He made a sound like sails snapping in a harsh wind and then fell forward, landing face down in the sand. Behind him, a familiar Shih-tzu stood, one paw clutching a fat coconut.

"Perfect timing, Goobriel," The Nose said. "Thought you were going to miss the chance to save my neck for a moment."

The Shih Tzu dropped the coconut, shook his head, and looked at her with dark, tear-stained eyes. "Not likely," he said. "Been waiting here for ages now."

The Nose nodded and gave the unconscious Hellbound a firm shove into the empty pit. It was not nearly deep enough to hold him, but then, he'd be sleeping for some time after a blow to the head like that.

"It was a nice trick with the blood," The Nose said. "How'd you sort that out?"

"Luck," he answered, wagging his waterfall tail. "Just happened to leap atop a good-sized fish. Then whick-whack with the boot knife and . . ."

"And you were dead." The Nose sniffed the air, but she smelled only a faint trace of blood on the little dog. "Is the gold loaded?"

"Yes, Cap'n," he said. "And the second yawl has conveniently sprung a leak."

"Well done." The Nose inhaled and turned her nose seaward. If Hellbound had left his men in the rocks to dig, they still had time to steal the mongrel's ship. She waved a grand gesture toward the outside of the atoll. "Shall we?"

"After you, Cap'n," Goob said.

They marched across the sandy stretch, to the place where Hellbound's yawls had been beached. One of them held her treasure. It would be a task for just the two of them to row back to the *Shrike*, but it wasn't like they had to rush. Not with a hefty hole scoring the bottom of the second boat.

She watched her first mate climb into the boat, settling in beside the treasure he'd fetched and loaded for her. "They didn't rough you up too much, did they?"

"Naw, Cap'n." Goob shook his head until his ears flopped. "I'm tougher than that lot."

"Yes, you are." She lay her shoulder against the yawl's prow and heaved it toward the waves again. "And I'm mighty glad to have you back."

"The rest of the crew?" Goob used an oar to assist her, and they slipped into the brine.

The Nose leapt aboard at the last moment, and they were off.

"Drinking themselves stupid in Canisport," she said, taking up a set of rows and heaving to. "We'll pick them up on the way out again."

"Din' expect you to come for me." He said it softly, low enough she had to stretch to hear him. "After I lost the map n'all."

"Silly," The Nose said.

"When I saw the *Widowmaker* go down . . ." he trailed off, and they both took a long look at the distant waves, at the silhouette of a ship that was not the *Widow* but was theirs just the same.

Finally, The Nose cleared her throat. "She was getting old, you know. Time for a change anyway. Besides, a ship's not made of wood and canvas, Goob. It's made of the blood, sweat, and tears of its crew. That there's the *Widowmaker* as much as any vessel. Or she will be once we fetch the rest of our pack."

"Aye, Cap'n," Goob said. "She'll do."

"She will," The Nose agreed.

They leaned into the oars, with the atoll behind them and their new ship ahead. Between them, a battered old chest full of treasure lay, a golden parcel wrapped in pirate tradition. Safe now, like Goob was. Both dogs looked upon their bounty with dark, shining eyes.

"What's it smell like?" Goob asked her.

"Family, Goobriel," The Nose said. "It smells like family."

Artistic Appropriation

George Jacobs

THE GUIDE WAVED the tour group, Buccleuch amongst them, into the next room with a shake of her antennae. It was wide and high-ceilinged and filled with a dizzying profusion of artefacts. Chitagasian war ladles glistened in glass cabinets, their bowls darkly stained by the blood of long dead foes. On one shelf sat an entire set of Lugoso bug-currency; on another a collection of matrixed light-sculptures from the fabled Ixon 9. The whole room seemed to crackle with strange and ancient wonder.

"This is perhaps the most famous exhibition in the whole museum," said the guide. Some of the group nodded or mumbled assent. It was true, it was famous.

"You have been dazzled by the wonders of the Oikune Continuum, past and present. You have seen feats of scientific and artistic achievement, the fruits of our most illustrious ancestors and a testament to the power and nobility of our Oikii spirit." The guide smiled, and Buccleuch thought she looked rather self-satisfied. Her role was an honourable one and she was richly if elegantly attired, with a refined accent. Most of the tour group, meanwhile, were simply dressed and spoke in what was considered lowborn fashion; they were country people on a rare trip to the High Capital, eager for a glimpse of the majesty and myth of an empire that each visitor felt a part of, in their own small way. All of them hung on the guide's every word and she knew it. All but one. Buccleuch alone paid little heed to her speech, his attention was already elsewhere.

"This room, too, is a testament to that power and nobility, though in a different way. For though you have seen many wonders in the other rooms, they all shared something: they were built by Oikii hands, conceived by Oikii minds. Not so the treasures here. No, my friends. These artefacts have far stranger origins. Each is the product of a culture either naturally extinct, subjected by the Continuum, or, in some rare and dangerous cases, exterminated entirely by the might of the Oikii. This is our Barbarian Room." She paused a moment to let the group gasp and caw; evidently, she had her routine down to a fine art. "Go, go," she shooed them. "Explore, enjoy. I will be here to answer any questions."

The group dispersed, heading towards whatever items most caught their attention. The strange and crude weapons of a dozen different worlds proved as popular as ever, and many of the Oikii posed awkwardly for photos beside the display cases, hefting replica blasters and draping themselves in foam armour. Yet, the humble pots of Firsk also had their admirers, as did the marriage rugs of Norn. One young woman pulled out a notepad and started sketching a set of erotic friezes. Buccleuch weaved between the tourists eager to see the famous relics, and headed for an otherwise empty corner of the room.

The item that held his attention was a little scrap of a thing, a picture composed of oil and crushed pigment depicting seven furred Terran creatures playing a primitive game. He pressed his face close to the glass, a feeling of awe building within him. In his chest, his heart beat just a little faster.

"I see you have an eye for the unusual."

Buccleuch jumped and turned to find the guide standing beside him. He coughed and smoothed his face tentacles but didn't say anything. He wore a heavy coat and an elegant head sculpture, giving an appearance that he hoped conjured just the right impression of class without placing expectation upon him that he would be familiar with the more intricate aspects of Oikii courtly society.

"The creatures here depicted are dogs, a type of companion

animal from a planet once known as Earth," continued the guide. "And I believe the game they are playing was called poker, a kind of gambling sport played with thin rectangles of paper. Not one of our more popular pieces, I must admit. Though interesting in its own way. Are you interested in Earth history?"

Buccleuch nodded.

"You must be quite the history aficionado then. I'm sorry to say that many of our visitors," she cast a glance at the other Oikii, who were marvelling at the jewel encrusted Royal Toilet of the once great Vestibuol Kingdom, "are not well versed in matters of learning. I doubt any of these others have even heard of Earth, or its Humans, for it is many millennia since they were expunged."

"Little was left of them after the Oikii purified their system," replied Buccleuch. His voice came out rough and halting, and he did his best to modulate it.

"True enough. They were a crude people."

"But creative," countered Buccleuch, gesturing at the painting. "And fond of their pets."

The guide shifted a tentacle in a wry smile. The keeping of companion animals was not well regarded amongst the Oikii.

"They were dangerous and brave too," said Buccleuch. "They destroyed three Oikii Navy Legions before . . ."

"Before being utterly destroyed. Yes, that's true." The guide pointed to a wall graphic that illustrated an Oikii naval fleet in all its combative might, and Buccleuch suppressed a shiver. "Through trickery and deceit they had some success—they fought in a most uncivilised manner. Yet in the end it did them no good and their species was destroyed by characteristic genephage."

Buccleuch frowned, creating a complex expression on his tentacled face, and the guide gave him a sidelong look. "You seem a bit of a xenophile. I hope you're not one of those conspiracy types," she said, "one of those believers in lost worlds and hidden aliens. Perhaps you still believe in the Pegasaurusi and Mother Winter too?"

"No, I don't believe that," replied Buccleuch. "But other creatures were left alive on Earth, were they not? Creatures such as these 'dogs', as you called them."

"Indeed, I presume they did survive, along with the plants and fungi of the world, if they were able to without their Human masters. The Oikii government is not cruel, and I hope you are not implying that. But, with the warlike Humans destroyed, Earth presented no threat to us. They, and their culture, are now just a footnote in our history, albeit an interesting one."

Before Buccleuch could respond, the lights in the room went out. The lights in the rooms surrounding were also out. A few people shouted or screamed, behaving a little over-dramatically, and a shrill alarm began to ring.

The guide's voice cut through the rising cacophony, "Please remain calm. I said *calm!*" She reached out all four arms to grab the nearest people and pushed them towards the dim orange light of the emergency exit, before taking hold of several wrists and dragging their owners after her. "Follow me, please, that's it. Everything's fine." Her voice trailed away into the darkness.

The room was quiet, but not empty. The solitary Buccleuch had avoided the grasping hands of the guide, and he remained before the painting, his gaze now returning to the little image of the poker playing dogs. He began to smile. It was a smile like one of the dogs in the painting, and it looked very strange on the chitinous Oikii face. It felt damned uncomfortable too, but Buccleuch could not risk removing his disguise till he was safely back aboard his ship and beyond the reach of the Continuum.

He opened his heavy coat and took out the glass-cutting tool. This wasn't his first theft, and in a moment the painting was out of its museum case and in a special holder nestled within the confines of the coat. In its place he had placed a decent facsimile that would buy him some time.

His canine eyes saw much better in the low light than did those of the Oikii, and he quickly caught up with the gaggle of evacuating people. Once outside the museum, Buccleuch milled around in the wide street with the rest of the crowd for a while, gawping and gossiping. He even asked a Gendarme what had caused the power outage, as if he didn't know. Then, having played the part well enough, he slipped away through the back alleys and out to the merchants' dockyard.

Entering his ship and securing the blast door behind him, Buccleuch O'Bassett could at last remove his disguise. He pulled off the tentacles and chitin that had given him the appearance of an Oikii, revealing a brown furred face, with a stubby snout and a wet nose. Next, he hung up the heavy coat and removed the stolen painting, placing it in next to the other artefacts he had already liberated. Items from Earth's past, depicting humanity and their dogs. And this last one, *A Friend in Need*, was the centrepiece.

Buccleuch O'Bassett smiled. The humans may be gone, but they were not forgotten. Not while the descendants of their pets lived on, having grown in intelligence and ability over the millennia since the war with the Oikii. Dog society prized anything that connected them to the humans, who had reared their species in ages long past.

Buccleuch settled himself down into the control chair of his ship and, with another self-satisfied smile on his face, set a course for New Earth, a world hidden in an outer arm of the galaxy well outside of Oikii space. With a haul of Earth artefacts as good as this, the Canid Council was sure to richly reward him.

WHAT FRISKY WROUGHT WHEN THE WHEELS FELL OFF THE WORLD

E.C. BELL

IN THE FOURTH month of the Sickness, Lucky and I were taking the sun in the backyard when a crow fluttered down onto the grass. I lifted my head, in order to guess the bird's intentions, but all it did was glare, unblinking.

"There's a bird," I finally said. "Staring at us."

"Well, chase it off," Lucky replied. "The backyard is ours, after all."

When my Chosen had let us out an hour before, I'd run to the big dog bed on the deck before Lucky could get to it, and I didn't want to lose my spot. "Why don't you?" I asked.

"Because I'm the Queen of the Pirates," she growled softly, her eyes still closed, "and I'll take you by the throat and shake you to death if you don't."

Since she was barely a third my size, I wasn't too worried about her shaking me to death, but I was surprised to hear her call herself the Queen of the Pirates. It had been months since

149

she'd even mentioned that name.

When I first met her, she'd been running with a pack of abandoned pets in the bush-choked valley that surrounded the North Saskatchewan River. Frisky, a German Shepard who'd washed out of cop school, played at being the Alpha of the pack, but everyone knew Lucky was the brains behind that particular crown. She was also sick, which was why I'd agreed to take her home with me. I knew the Owner and my Chosen could help her get well.

Lucky had promised the pack she'd come back when she was well. However, part of getting well entailed having many of her teeth removed, which meant a long time for recovery. So, days away from the pack became weeks.

Then the Sickness hit the Humans, and we were trapped. Humans and Beings, trapped inside. Never going walkies. Hardly ever smelling the outside past the backyard. The Owner and my Chosen watched the news on the television, instead of the movies Lucky loved, and fretted about what was happening outside the four walls where we hid.

Lucky and I spent our time napping, for the most part. She told me stories, because that was Lucky's way. First, she told me stories of the pack, and then she told me about the lives of pirates, free and wild.

"We could be that," she'd said, from her spot on the couch.

"Be what?" I asked.

"Pirates," she said. "You and me and the pack. We could all be pirates. And I would be the Queen, again. The Queen of the Pirates."

She'd based most of her research on the movies she'd watched with her original Owner, and most of it sounded quite unbelievable to me, but because it seemed to make her happy, I let her talk.

Eventually, she stopped telling me the stories. And then, she stopped planning our escape back to the pack. We became Pets again and I for one was glad of it. Living rough had been horrible and I most definitely did not want to be a pirate. Not if it meant going on the water, which I hated.

However, she had been the Queen of the Pirates when I first met her, and those titles don't fall away just because time passes and teeth are removed.

I groaned, like I was terribly inconvenienced, and rose to chase away the crow. As I stepped onto the lawn, Lucky scurried over and settled on my still-warm bed, just like I knew she would.

"Get out of here!" I growled at the crow, who did nothing but ruffle his feathers. I glanced at Lucky, but her eyes were already closed.

"He won't leave," I said.

"Then kill him," Lucky replied. "I would, but I think you need the exercise."

Killing a crow for trespassing is hard, even for a Being as fast and driven as a Border Collie. Crows can fly, after all. And since I was a Tripod, I was pretty sure I wouldn't catch him before he took off. And honestly? The thought of killing the bird didn't appeal to me. I wasn't hungry, and all he was doing was staring at us.

"Get out of here," I said, again. "The Queen says you have to go."

The bird blinked and flapped his wings. "The Queen?" he cawed, his accent so strong I could barely understand him. "Have I finally found the Queen of the Pirates?"

I'd had about as much as I could stand of the smartass bird, and was going to run at him, gnashing my teeth and growling deep in my throat, but Lucky stopped me by answering the bird herself.

"I am," she said, from her warm spot on my bed. "Why are you looking for me?"

"The coyotes asked us to find you," the bird said, hopping a couple of feet closer to Lucky, and ignoring me. "You have to come back to the boat."

I glanced at Lucky. That bird was talking about the *Edmonton Queen*, a riverboat that had been used by the Humans as amusement before the Sickness overtook the world. That boat was where we'd left Lucky's pack of abandoned pets the winter before. It had also figured prominently in Lucky's pirate stories.

"Why?" she asked.

"Because Frisky the Fearless is causing problems," the crow said.

"Frisky the who?" Lucky asked.

"The Fearless," the bird answered, hopping a few steps closer to Lucky and staring with his bright beady eyes. "We've heard stories from the dogs who have escaped Frisky's pack. Stories about the Queen of the Pirates. How she was small but mighty and could control him with a word. You have to come back. You have to stop him, before this all gets out of hand."

Lucky stood. "What's he been doing?"

"He's been—marauding," the crow said. "He and his crew take on anyone—everyone—who passes through their territory. They drove off the cats, and that was good, but now they kill with impunity, and the coyotes have had just about as much as they can stand. There will be a war if he isn't stopped. A war will attract the attention of the Humans, and that will mean horror for all of us."

The crow lowered his head and flapped his wings in an awkward bow. "Please tell me you're the Queen I seek," he said. "And that you can stop this maniac."

Lucky stared at the bird, and I stared at Lucky. All she had to do was flash me a sign, and I'd be on him as quick as a minute since he was standing nearly at my feet, but she closed her eyes and shook her head.

"I guess I always knew this day would come," she muttered.

She stretched and shook out her hair, clipped close for the summer. Then she stepped delicately onto the grass, and came nose to beak with the crow. "Go and tell the coyotes that you found the Queen," she said. "I'll stop Frisky."

The crow bowed one last time, and then took off, his wings beating the air. As he disappeared from view, I turned on Lucky, teeth bared.

"I thought you said we were done with that life," I growled. "We're retired. You know how upset the Owner and my Chosen will be if we disappear again—"

"I know," she snapped. "But the pack is my responsibility. I have to stop Frisky." She sat and scratched her ear, absently. "You don't have to come if you don't want to. I know it's difficult for you. Getting around like that."

She stared pointedly at my stump. A Vet from the Place That Smells had removed my back leg before I became a Pet, and I felt a flash of fury.

"I can travel as well as anyone," I snarled. "You know that. I saved you, after all."

"The Owner and your Chosen saved my life by taking me to

the Vet," Lucky replied with a sharp laugh. "And you know it."

I shrugged, because she had spoken the truth. I'd brought her home, but the Owner and my Chosen had done the actual healing. "Do you promise we'll be back soon?" I asked.

"Yes," Lucky said. "It won't take long to stop Frisky. He's stupid, but not stupid enough to want a war with the Coyotes. He knows that will bring on the vengeance of the Humans. He's been to the Place That Smells and barely escaped with his life. He won't want to go back."

"Then I'll go with you," I sighed. "We'll stop Frisky the Fearless together, and then we'll come home."

I hoped.

WE LEFT THAT night. Breaking out was easy, because my Chosen never found the hole in the fence I'd used when I'd run away in the winter. We headed to the park and hit the trails that led to the river. We hid when we saw the few Humans who ventured out, and we hid when we saw Beings walking alone. We did not want word getting back to Frisky before we were ready to talk to him.

We also saw Coyotes, but they steered clear of us. Just watching, always watching.

"They're giving me the creeps," I said, when we passed three more of them sitting by a fence, staring. "Can't we run them off or something?"

"They aren't going to hurt us," Lucky said.

"How can you be so sure?" I asked.

"They expect us—me—to stop Frisky," she said. "It wouldn't be in their best interests to stop us before we do that, would it?"

"No," I conceded.

"So, keep your head down, and let's get to the river," she said. And so we did.

WE SAW NO Beings when we got to the river valley. We could smell where they'd marked their territory, though. It was much larger than it had been when Lucky and I had left, months before. Frisky had been busy.

No wonder the coyotes wanted him stopped. It smelled like he'd taken huge chunks of their territory.

We walked under an old bridge that crossed the river to the Down of the Town, where all was concrete and wind and no sane animals ventured. In the distance we saw the boat—the *Edmonton Queen*—where we'd left the pack the winter before. It was still moored to the dock, haphazardly, even though the river was running.

The Sickness had stopped it, too.

But we saw no Beings. None at all. "So, this is strange, right?" I finally asked

"It is," she said. "You'd think we'd find a patrol, at the very least. But nothing. I don't understand."

We found spoor of Beings. That, and bones, scattered over the floor of valley. Lots and lots of bones. Rabbit and bird and small cat, mostly, but other bones, too.

"Are those the bones of our own?" I asked, horrified.

"I hope not," Lucky said. "They might be coyote, but I'm not sure."

But we did not see any Beings anywhere. Not alive.

WE FOLLOWED A scent trail to the dock, where the *Edmonton Queen* was moored. Just one chain haphazardly held it, and I could see that the river's current was catching the boat, moving it, trying to pull it free.

"That doesn't look safe," I muttered. Lucky ignored me and walked onto the dock. She demand-barked at the boat, her tail waving in the night breeze like a white and black flag.

"Parlay!" she cried, boldly. "Parlay!"

Two Beings, obviously guards, popped their heads up. When they caught sight of her, they stalked to the side of the boat closest to the dock. A plank, narrow and scary-looking, stretched from the side of the boat to the dock, but they did not descend to our level.

Lucky glared at them. "I demand a parlay," she said again. "Now."

"How do you know that word?" one of them finally asked.

"Because I'm the Queen of the Pirates," Lucky said. "Of course."

The bigger of them squinted at her, a half grin of nervousness on his face. "Lucky?" he finally said. "Is that you?"

"Of course it's me," she said, and sniffed the air. "And you're Spot. Right?"

"Right," Spot said. "You smell so Human, we thought the men

had come back."

"Men?" Lucky asked.

"They were here the night before, and said they're taking the boat, once they remove that last chain." Spot grinned again, afraid. "We don't know how to stop them. And Frisky's been gone for a while now."

"Where is he?" Lucky asked.

"He's gone to get the Lucy, or so he says," Spot replied.

Lucky gasped, and took a small step back, the flag of her tail wilting. "He's gone where?"

"To the zoo," Spot said. "To get the Lucy. You know. According to the plan."

"Oh no," she muttered. "He wouldn't be that stupid."

"What are they talking about?" I asked. "What's a Lucy?"

Lucky snuck a glance at me. "Frisky is in the process of doing a bad thing," she finally said. "A truly stupid thing." She turned to the guards. "You do understand that the idea is a bad one, don't you?"

Spot raised a lip. "Frisky listened to you," he said. "He listened to everything you said. And he figures it'll work."

A pup showed its face over the side of the boat and grinned at us. Then another face appeared, and another.

"Bernard, get them back!" Spot yelled, and an ancient Being, all rheumy eyes and slobbery jowls, slowly lifted his giant body from wherever he'd evidently been sleeping.

"Aye aye, Spot," he said. Then, the pups yipped in fear and disappeared to the far side of the boat, and we were alone again.

"Why are pups on board?" Lucky asked. "And where is the rest of the pack?"

The guards glanced at each other nervously, then Spot glowered down at her. "What's going on here is none of your concern," he said. "Not anymore."

"I'm the Queen—" Lucky started again, but Spot cut off her words with a snarl.

"You left," he said. "Frisky the Fearless is the one true leader now. We listen to him. Just him. He'll be back soon, with the Lucy, and then he's going to save us from the Humans. Just like you said you were going to do, before you left us."

Lucky licked her lips and shook her head. "I had to heal," she finally said.

"You abandoned us," Spot said. "And you know it."

Then he bristled and set a foot on the plank. "You are a usurper, and we're not listening to anything you say any longer. Go, before we call the Hounds of Hell down on you."

Lucky frowned. "The Hounds of Hell?"

"Frisky's cohort," Spot said. "He came up with that name himself."

"So, it's Frisky the Fearless and the Hounds of Hell," Lucky continued. "That's who you're following now?"

"At least he stayed!" Spot bayed. "He fed us. He's trying to make life better for us. We don't need you anymore!"

He tipped his head and began to howl. After a few seconds, the other guard joined him, and then a couple of the pups joined the song.

"Are they calling Frisky?" I asked. From down the river valley, we heard another howl. And then another, rebounding off the cliffs and away.

"I don't know, but I think we should regroup," Lucky said. "Let's go."

We ran off, stopping in the boneyard to catch our breath. "We're not going to be able to take them all on," I said. "Not if they're committed to Frisky."

"I know," Lucky said. "That's why I want to talk to the coyotes. See if they'll help us."

"That feels treasonous," I muttered. "Consorting with coyotes."

"We're here to stop Frisky because the coyotes want him stopped," Lucky said. "The least they can do is lend us a hand."

She walked away from me before I could answer, and then barked twice, sharply. It didn't take long before a coyote coalesced before us.

"Is it done?" he asked. "That didn't take long."

"I don't think we'll be able to stop Frisky," Lucky said. "Not alone. He's taken his crew to the zoo."

Three more coyotes appeared, like smoke. "The zoo?" one of them asked. "That place is evil. Why would they go there?"

"To get the Lucy. An elephant," Lucky replied.

"A what?" I asked.

"An elephant," Lucky said. "The Humans call her the Lucy. A massive beast that should be living on the other side of the world.

She was kidnapped and brought here ages ago, when she was a pup, to entertain the Humans. Some of them think she should be released." She licked her lips. "My Human did, anyhow."

I could feel the sudden despair flow from her. It happened whenever she talked about the Owner who had come before. Lucky had been with her since she was a pup, but when that Owner died, Lucky had been left to her own devices. An abandoned Pet, which was how she ended up with the pack, and with Frisky.

"How big is this . . . elephant?" one of the coyotes asked. "As big as a bison? I've heard bisons are huge beasts—as tall as trees—who could feed a pack for a long time. If they can be brought down."

He huffed and glared when the rest of the coyotes chittered laughter.

"There are no beasts that big," one said.

"My cousin told me," the first replied, snarling. "They saw a herd of bison, beyond a fence, when she and her mate were coming to the city. They are really big. Maybe not as tall as a tree, but big, all the same."

"The elephant is bigger," Lucky replied.

"Bigger than Randolph's cousin's magical bison?" another coyote sneered. "Are you serious?"

"I'm serious," Lucky said. "I saw her, once. Walking in the zoo. She's as tall as a building, and the rage that seethes just below the surface of that Being is something to feel. She could do the job, if she could get free."

"What job?" the big coyote asked.

"She could go into the river and pull the *Edmonton Queen* free from its moorings," Lucky replied. "Set it free, for Frisky and his Dogs of Doom, or whatever."

"How did Frisky find out about the elephant?" I asked.

"From me," Lucky replied, mournfully. "From my stories. They were for the pups, but he listened. And now, he's following them, to the letter."

I thought of all the stories she'd told me, while we were trapped in the house with our Humans. Wild tales of us as pirates, using the *Edmonton Queen* to take over the world. I couldn't remember her ever talking about an elephant named the Lucy, But then, I'd slept through a lot of her stories. However, it sounded like Frisky had listened, and believed. Completely.

The coyotes milled around, talking nervously among themselves. Finally, the largest one stepped forward. "We're not going to the zoo," he said. "Not even to stop those dogs. That place is evil. The craziness of the Beings within poisons the air around it for miles." He shook his head. "We're not going there."

"You don't have to," Lucky said, sadly. "Frisky's on a suicide mission. That place is a fortress. If he makes it there, the Humans will stop them."

"Then we have nothing more to worry about," the coyote said. "The humans will eliminate our problem, and it shouldn't come back on us."

"But, the boat," Lucky yipped. "There are pups on board, with two guards. Help me save them."

"Not our problem either," the coyote said. "You should be able to deal with two guards. Save them yourselves."

Lucky was going to lose it on him, when a coyote guarding the perimeter chirped a warning.

"Dogs coming," he yipped. "Might be Frisky and the Hounds of Hell."

"I thought you said the Humans would kill him," the biggest coyote yowled angrily. He stood over Lucky, menacing her. To give her credit, she didn't move a muscle. Just stared at him until he finally took a small step back.

"I said the Humans would finish them if they got to the zoo," Lucky growled back. "Looks like he didn't get that far." She sneered. "Why didn't your pack smell him, if he was so close?"

"I don't know," the coyote said, and groaned. "Son of a bitch. This is the last thing any of us wanted."

"Just give me some back up, so I can save the pups," Lucky said. "That's all I need."

"I don't think so," the coyote said. "Frisky'll want to fight, and a fight will bring the Humans. We can't have Humans after us. No. He's your problem, not ours."

We watched in horror as the coyotes melted back into the trees, disappearing from our view.

"Well," Lucky muttered. "Looks like we're on our own."

"Can you stop Frisky?" I asked.

"I'll do my best," she replied. "If you have my back."

"Always," I replied. "After all, you're the Queen of the Pirates.

Right?"

"Right," she said.

But the for the first time since I'd known her, she didn't sound certain, and my heart pounded with sudden fear. We were on our own against Frisky and his Hounds of Hell, and I was suddenly afraid that it could mean our deaths.

I HAVE GOOD ears, but I didn't hear Frisky until he, surrounded by his Hounds of Hell, ran through the trees into the boneyard.

It looked to me as though Frisky had grown by half. His face was covered in fight scars, and the snarl on his lips looked permanent. The rest of his Hounds of Hell looked just as well-fed, well-scarred, and well-muscled, but they stopped when they saw us, and stared intently.

Frisky threw back his head and laughed. "Well look at that," he said. "The Tripod is back. I thought you were dead."

"Not yet," I replied. I was surprised he'd spoken to me first. After all, Lucky was standing beside me, and she was the Queen of the Pirates.

"Who's the bitch?" Frisky asked, finally glancing at Lucky. "Your mother?"

He didn't recognize her.

His cohort laughed roughly, but before I could make a move, Lucky bristled. "Watch your language, Frisky," she snarled.

Frisky blinked in surprise and sniffed the air, furiously. "Lucky?" he finally asked. "Is that really you?"

"Yes," Lucky said.

"You smell Human," Frisky said.

"So I've been told," Lucky replied.

"I assumed you were dead, too."

"Well, I'm not," Lucky said, shortly. "As you can see."

"You didn't come back," he said, and then coughed as though a bone had caught in his throat. "You promised you'd come back, Lucky."

"I know," Lucky said, and I could hear guilt in her voice. "I shouldn't have left you alone, Frisky. I'm sorry."

"The Fearless," Frisky said, his voice rough. "It's Frisky the Fearless now."

He shook his head, suddenly angry, and glared at both of us. His cohort stiffened, and I could see the hair standing on their necks. We were in trouble here. Serious trouble.

"Maybe we should go," I whispered, but Lucky shook off my words. Just kept her eyes on Frisky, and took a step toward him.

"I'm back now, though," she said. "And we have to talk. What you're planning—it's not going to work. You have to understand that."

Frisky snarled, and jerked his head in the direction of the *Edmonton Queen,* just visible through the clots of bush clinging to the river's edge. "Remember what you said?" he asked. "'All we need is a ship, and a star to steer her by.' You said that. Remember?"

"I remember," she sighed.

"Well, we have the ship," Frisky said, and then pointed to the sky with his snout. "And there are the stars. We're set. Once we get to the zoo and free the Lucy."

"Spot told me that's where you were going," Lucky said. "What happened?"

Frisky grinned, as if embarrassed. "It's further away than we realized," he said. "I thought it would only take one night to get there, but it took longer. We had to hide out until the sun set again, and then we had to eat."

His Hounds of Hell chuckled, evilly, and I wondered what they'd found and eaten. More Beings? Other Pets?

"So you didn't get very far away," Lucky said. "There's still a chance to turn this around. Stop the madness."

"Tomorrow, we'll head out again," Frisky said, as though Lucky hadn't spoken. "This time we'll get to the zoo and set the elephant free. Then she'll push the boat into the river, and we'll head downstream, gathering other Beings as we go. Soon, we'll reach the ocean. And from there, the world is ours."

"Frisky, those were just stories I told the pups as they were settling in to sleep," Lucky said, softly. "You have to understand that. The Humans will never let you do any of that."

"The Humans are finished!" he roared. "They're sick, and disappearing. We see fewer and fewer of them, every day. Soon, we'll have the world to ourselves, and we can finally run it. Our way."

His cohort lifted their snouts and howled, and I felt the hair stand on my back. They no longer sounded like pets, even abandoned ones. Now, they sounded wild, and I was afraid she'd lost them all.

"The humans aren't disappearing," Lucky said, over the howls. Her voice sounded so steady I was impressed. "They've just gone into hiding, is all. And what you're doing—all the killing—is going to attract their attention, eventually. Sooner, if you go to the zoo. You'll all end up in the Place With the Smell, and you won't survive this time."

"That's a lie!" Frisky roared. "The Humans are almost gone! We're nearly free!"

"They aren't," Lucky said. "They're just hiding until the Sickness is over. That's all."

"And how do you know that?" Frisky snarled.

"Because I've seen it with my own eyes," Lucky said. She jerked her head in my direction. "His people—his Chosen, and the Owner—that's what they're doing. Hiding until the Sickness is over. But then they'll be back."

"Is—is that true?" a deep voice intoned, from the back of Frisky's cohort.

"It is," Lucky said. "And not all of them are hiding. Humans are still moving around. Some have even been to the *Edmonton Queen*. Go ask Spot, if you don't believe me."

"You're lying!" Frisky roared.

He crouched, suddenly prepared to attack, and I growled, deep in my throat. "Leave her alone," I said. "She's telling you the truth."

"I don't believe anything she says," he replied. "Not anymore." He flicked his head at his cohort. "Get rid of them," he said. "Get rid of them both."

The Hounds of Hell stepped closer, growling so low it made the hair stand on my back, and that was when the coyotes appeared through the trees and bush, like acrid smoke, bristling and growling deep in their own throats.

I had never been so happy to see a coyote in my life.

The Hounds of Hell yipped and stepped back, staring at all the coyotes flooding in around them. It looked like every coyote in Edmonton was there.

"It appears we're getting a war whether we want it or not," the coyote leader said to Lucky. "We're going to finish this, now, and then we're clearing out. Frisky has made this too dangerous for all of us."

"And after the fight, we're going to see the bison," Randolph said, grinning.

"Yes," the big coyote said with a sigh. "Yes, we are." Then he laughed. "There are idiots everywhere," he said to Lucky. "Aren't there?"

"Yes," she said. "There are."

"Go save those pups, if you can," he said. "And we'll finish the Hounds of Hell."

"Thank you," Lucky said. And then we turned tail and ran.

I saw that two coyotes were following us, as coyotes and dogs threw themselves at each other in a sudden clash of violence. The screaming and growling was almost more than I could bear, and I turned on them, prepared to at least keep Lucky safe.

"We're not fighting you!" I cried. "Don't you understand that?"

"We do," one of the coyotes said. "We're here to help you with the pups. They're innocent in all this. They don't deserve to die."

I blinked, surprised, as the coyotes ran past me, following Lucky to the boat. And then, I brought up the rear.

The sounds of the fierce fight faded as we travelled through the bush back to the boat. Then we stopped, because the smell of Human hung thick in the air. Three men stood on the dock, hacking away at the final chain that held the *Edmonton Queen* secure.

"Hurry up," one of them said, and then starting coughing, a long hard hack that sounded like he was losing a lung. I suspected he had the Sickness, and felt the hair on my back stiffen.

"Gimme a break," the one wielding the axe replied. "This chain is thick."

He swung the axe, and there was a metallic chonk as he connected. "Do something about those dogs on board," he said. "While I work on this."

"What do you expect me to do?" the cougher asked.

"Kill 'em," the man with the axe said. "And throw them overboard."

"Hell, yeah." The third man cackled wildly. "Kill them all."

I looked at Lucky. "We have to save those pups," I said. "But we can't hurt the Humans, or we'll end up in the Place With the Smell. You know that."

"I don't care," she growled. "I've had my fill of idiots for one day."

One of the coyotes snorted laughter, quieting only when she turned on him, glaring.

"They're not hurting those pups," she said. "Let's go."

We slunk up to the dock, surrounding it as the man with the axe hit the chain holding the boat a final time. The chain slumped and splashed into the water, and the man cheered.

"I did it!" he said. "Now get rid of those dogs, so we can get the hell out of here."

"But—but they're puppies," the guy with the cough said. "I'm not killing puppies. Why don't we sell them?"

"We don't have time for that," the guy with the axe said. "Wilbur's waiting for this thing, down river. Throw them overboard if you're too chicken to kill them by hand."

The two men scrabbled up the plank that stretched from the side of the boat to the dock. When they dropped into the boat, Spot appeared, growling and stalking toward them. The guy with the cough screeched in fear and scrabbled back to the plank.

"We need help," he squalled, falling all over himself in his fear, and we watched in horror as the plank wobbled and nearly fell. "There are three big dogs here. They looks dangerous."

"We need that plank," I said. "Or we won't be able to get the pups back to land."

"Then we attack now," Lucky said, and leaped forward, growling and facing the man with the axe.

He stared at her for what felt like forever, and then laughed in her face. "You're a frigging Shih Tzu," he finally said, and raised the axe over his head. "What do you think you're going to do?"

"She thinks she's going to save her own!" I howled, and threw myself at the man, knocking him off balance. He flailed frantically, and then fell into the river with a splash and a scream. The current caught him and pulled him downstream, still screaming and then choking as the water covered him.

I turned to Lucky. "We have to hurry. He might not drown."

"Well, I didn't think you had it in you," Lucky said, grinning at me before scrambling up the plank to the deck of the boat. I followed, shuddering. Knocking a Human into the water was dangerous, but the plank? It was terrifying.

I felt it wobble, and I pancaked, feeling such fear I could barely move. The two coyotes who had come with us leaped over me, growling at me to get out of the way. Then they faced down the two men who were still on the boat.

"Jesus," one of the men screeched. "What the hell is going on here? Those are coyotes!"

We heard a splash, and then another, and we listened to the men swim away from the boat.

Lucky looked down at me still cowering on the wobbling plank. "You coming?"

"Yeah," I said. "Just give me a second."

I stood slowly took a shuddering step, and then another. almost ready to piss with fear. There are two things I'm afraid of. An unsteady floor, and deep water. And there I was, dealing with both.

By the time I finally scrabbled up that plank, the two coyotes had Spot and the other guard backed onto the stern of the ship.

"Really?" Spot cried when he saw Lucky. "You've sided with the coyotes? You should be ashamed of yourself!"

"Screw you, Pet," one of the coyotes replied, "she knows the winning side."

We were seconds away from bloodshed when Lucky stepped between them. "The Humans are gone," she said. "But they'll be back. Nothing stops Humans once they've set their sights on something. If they want the boat, they will take the boat. You know that."

The guards cowered, finally silent.

"So go," she said. "We won't stop you. We're just here for the pups."

One of the coyotes stepped aside, and the two guards skittered past him, scrabbling down the plank and to the deck. From there they ran into the woods and disappeared.

"Are you good?" one of the coyotes said to Lucky. "Can you handle the pups? If you are, we're going back to warn our pack. The Humans will be back, and soon. We have to leave."

Lucky nodded, and the coyotes ran down the plank, disappearing in the direction of the dog/coyote clash.

When they were gone, she trotted up to the pups, who were still flailing and screaming in terror at the edge of the cabin. "Enough of the noise," she said sharply. "It's time for us to leave. Now."

They fell silent, then one by one scrabbled down the plank to the dock where they huddled together, as if for warmth. But the last pup cried in sudden terror and ran around the cabin, disappearing from our sight.

"Get him," Lucky said to me. "And find Bernard. He needs saving, too."

The pup that ran away was young. Too young to be without a mother. But there he was, alone and afraid, cowering beside an old Being who stood in the bow, stiff-legged with fear.

"Save me, Bernard," the pup wailed. "I'm so afraid."

I looked past the pup to the old Being. "Bernard, we have to go," I growled. "Right now."

"I'm one of the pirates," the old Being said, his eyes rolling in terror. "Frisky put me in charge of the waifs. Besides, I have arthritis, and that plank is terrifying. Just leave me here."

The pup squealed, "You can't stay, Bernard!"

"He's right," I said. "You can't stay. Frisky will kill you for letting the pups escape. So, let's call you my prisoner. We're all leaving. Now."

"Thank you," Bernard whispered, gratitude oozing from his old voice. He stood with a groan and scuttled toward the plank, and freedom. The squalling pup followed him, tail between his legs.

Bernard nosed the pup onto the plank, and he scuttled down to Lucky and the others. He left a trail of urine, and I hoped he hadn't made the plank slippery. Going up had been hard enough for me, but going down was going to be next to impossible, even without slipping in piss.

"Go," I said to Bernard, and he gamely stepped onto the plank, and then froze, his big frame shaking.

"I don't think I can," he said.

"Just go!" I barked, and gave him a push. He cried out in fear, and pancaked on the plank, as it wobbled dangerously.

"I can't," he gasped. "I just can't."

"Lucky!" I cried. "Help me move this old fool."

Lucky looked up from the pups. "Bernard?" she called. "Come on, you can make it. You know you can."

Movement at the top of the hill caught my eye. Beings, threading their way through the trees, toward us. It looked like the fight was over, and Frisky was coming to take us on, too.

"We have company," I said, urgently.

Lucky didn't look. Just grabbed Bernard by the jowl, and

pulled, hard. Not many teeth, but she used what she had, and Bernard squealed, pulling away from the pain.

The plank jiggled terrifically at his movement, and he half fell into the water by the dock. It took him a while to pull himself out, and then he shook, soaking everything with spray.

"Oh no," I whispered. The plank was still wobbling, and now it was covered in water. And Frisky and what remained of his Hounds of Hell were galloping down the hill toward us.

"Go!" I cried, and then took two steps back, and launched myself over the edge of the boat. I hoped I'd hit the dock, and I did, but my frantic kick-off threw me past it and into the river. The water closed over my head, and I knew then that I was done for. I was going to drown in that damned river. I was certain of it.

I might be able to run almost as fast as a Being with four legs, but I couldn't swim. I'd learned that horrible lesson almost drowning in a creek when my Chosen had taken me to the off-leash park, and that was the last time I'd let water close over my head.

Until now.

I fought and choked, and then someone grabbed the ruff at the back of my neck, like my mother had when I was still suckling. I was hauled onto the dock, choking on river water, but still alive.

I looked up into the rheumy eyes of Bernard, who was standing over me, grinning wildly through his dripping wet face fur.

"You saved me," I gasped.

"Well, you saved the Queen," Bernard said. "And now, you're helping her save the pups. So we're square." He pointed with his snout. "Go. Go with her. I'll keep Frisky occupied to give you time."

"Come with us," I said, frantically. "You can make it."

"I'm old," Bernard said. "And I can't run. But I can still fight. Go. Get them somewhere safe. I got your back."

Then he stood, growling, the ruff on his neck standing magnificently as he faced Frisky and the Hounds of Hell.

I scrabbled off the dock and ran after Lucky and the pups, who had already headed to the top of the hill, and over. I glanced back, once, and watched Bernard heroically keeping his word. He knocked two of the Hounds of Hell into the river, barking ferociously, before the rest of them fell on him, snarling and gnashing, and pulled him down.

The fight knocked the plank free, and the *Edmonton Queen* lurched away from the dock. Frisky saw the boat heading for open water and roared, leaping from the dock to the deck of the boat.

"Jump!" he called to the rest of the Hounds. Four of them made it before the current pulled the boat to the middle of the river.

The Beings who remained on the dock stood and stared in horror. "Come back for us!" one of them cried. "Frisky! You have to come back!"

Frisky shook his head. "I'm sorry, lads. You missed the boat." He snickered, and looked over at the four Beings who stood beside him. "Did you hear that?" he asked. "I said they missed the boat."

"You're hilarious, Fearless," a large Mastiff said, without a drop of humour. "Hilarious."

"And don't you forget it," Frisky snapped. Then he turned back to the Beings still milling around on the dock. "We'll come back for you," he called. "Once we've taken over the world."

"But—but what do we do until that happens?" one of them asked.

Frisky shrugged. "No clue," he said. "But try to make me proud." Then he walked to the bow of the ship, ignoring their cries for help, and stared out at the river before him.

"I am the Queen of the Pirates!" he cried, his voice echoing off the banks of the river. "I am finally the Queen of the Pirates and I'm going to take over the world!"

AT THE TOP of the ravine, I found Lucky waiting with the pups.

"Bernard?" she asked.

"He died a hero," I replied, and pointed with my muzzle at the *Edmonton Queen* lumbering down the river. "Frisky and his crew are on board the boat," I said. "Well, some of them, anyhow. The rest will be really angry. We should leave."

I heard a siren, off in the distance. A Human had called the Authorities. If we didn't get home, and soon, we'd all find ourselves in the Place With the Smell, where all bad Pets go to die.

As we ran past an open spot in the bush, I caught our last sight of the *Edmonton Queen*, with Frisky still at the bow, howling maniacally at the stars as they melted in the early morning sunrise.

"So, he's finally the Queen of the Pirates," Lucky said. "Good for him."

We heard another siren, and then a third. "We have to go," I said. "Right now."

Lucky nodded and turned the pups in the direction of the Owner and my Chosen, where we would all, finally, be safe.

"I hope he makes it to the ocean," Lucky said.

I looked at her, surprised. "Why?"

"Because if Frisky's on the ocean," she said. "We'll finally be safe from him. And oh, think of the stories we'll be able to tell."

I laughed, and shook my head. "I think we've heard enough stories for now," I said. "Let's get these guys home."

And so, we did.

BIOGRAPHIES

Rhonda Parrish
Editor

Like a magpie, Rhonda Parrish is constantly distracted by shiny things. She's the editor of many anthologies and author of plenty of books, stories, and poems (some of which have even been nominated for awards!). She lives in Edmonton, Alberta, and she can often be found there playing Dungeons and Dragons, bingeing crime dramas, making blankets, or cheering on the Oilers.

Her website, updated regularly, is at rhondaparrish.com and her Patreon, updated even more regularly, is at patreon.com/RhondaParrish.

Chadwick Ginther
The Empress of Marshmallow

Chadwick Ginther has over thirty years' experience getting bossed around by adorable floofs. This story wouldn't have existed without some very good girls (and one very good boy), his canine sisters and brother, Sasha, Nikita, Queisha, Ruby, and Rio. When he is not guarding his cheese from chow chows, Chadwick lives and writes in Winnipeg. He is the author of the Thunder Road Trilogy, *Graveyard Mind*, and over twenty short stories, including "All Cats Go to Valhalla" which won the 2021 Prix Aurora Award for Best Short Story.

Jennifer Lee Rossman
Davy Bones and the Domestication of the Dutchman

Jennifer Lee Rossman (she/they) is a queer, disabled, and autistic author and editor from the land of carousels and Rod Serling. Find more of their work on their website http://jenniferleerossman.blogspot.com and follow them on Twitter @JenLRossman

Meghan Beaudry
Johnson the Terror

Meghan Beaudry began writing as part of her rehabilitation from brain trauma in 2014 and simply never stopped. Her work has been published in *Hippocampus*, *Ravishly*, *Folks at Pillpack*, *Al Jazeera*, and the *Huffington Post*. She was nominated for a Pushcart Prize in 2017. In 2020, she was selected as winner of the Pen 2 Paper Creative Writing Contest in fiction. She blogs for Lupus.net.

Kristen Brand
Ghost Pirate Dognapper

If Kristen Brand could have any superpower, she'd want telekinesis so she wouldn't have to move from her computer to pour a new cup of tea. She lives in Florida with her husband, and her hobbies include reading comic books and desperately trying to keep the plants in her garden alive. An author of speculative fiction, she writes stories with fire-forged friends, explosive fight scenes, and kissing.

Richard Lau
Blackbark's Collar

Richard Lau has been "puglished" in magazines, newspapers, anthologies, and the high-tech industry. He navigates smoother seas, thanks to his first and best mate, Barbara.

V.F. LeSann
Let the Water Drink First

V.F. LeSann is the co-writing team of Leslie Van Zwol and Megan Fennell, united for greater power like Captain Planet, and sworn to tread the wobbly line between grit and whimsy. They are both great fans of pirates (despite being tragically landlocked) and of pups (despite owning one who shows affection primarily through high-fives to the face). Having been a part of the previous *Swashbuckling Cats* anthology, they were not about to miss the opportunity to put the "wag" in scallywag with this one.

Alice Dryden
New Tricks

Alice Dryden writes stories and poems about talking animals. Most of these are published in the furry fandom under the name Huskyteer, but occasionally one escapes into the wild. She edited the *Furry Megapack* for Wildside Press, and in 2019 she was Guest of Honor at Fur the 'More 007: Furry Never Dies. When not being a dog on the internet, she enjoys motorcycling, gin, karate, and open water swimming, though not all at the same time. You can find her at huskyteer.co.uk or on Twitter as @Huskyteer.

Melanie Marttila
Torvi, Viking Queen

Always looking up, eyes on the skies, head in the clouds, #actuallyautistic author Melanie Marttila writes poetry and speculative tales of hope in the face of adversity. She lives and writes in Sudbury, Ontario, in the house where three generations of her family have lived, on the street that bears her surname, with her spouse and their dog, Torvi.

Mathew Austin
Under the Curse of Jupiter

Mathew Austin has a Master's degree in Creative Writing from Kingston University. He previously worked for a media trust contributing to the production of environmental films broadcast on BBC World. He now hangs art exhibitions and spends his time writing in London.

JB Riley
The Boomer Bust

JB Riley writes and edits technical healthcare proposals for a major US-based corporation, but has loved reading and writing speculative fiction ever since discovering The Chronicles of Narnia at age eight. When not trawling the shelves at the local bookstore, she enjoys travel, hockey, beer, and cooking. JB lives in Chicago with her family; which currently includes an eighty-pound dog, a puppy the size of a bathtub who thinks he's a lapdog, a fifteen-pound cat, and a five-pound cat that scares the hell out of everyone.

Frances Pauli
What Gold Smells Like

Frances Pauli writes books about animals, hybrids, aliens, shifters, and occasionally ordinary humans. She tends to cross genre boundaries, but hovers around fantasy and science fiction with romantic tendencies.

Her work has won four Leo awards, two Coyotl awards, and has been nominated for an Ursa Major award.

She lives in Washington State with her family, a small menagerie, and far too many houseplants.

George Jacobs
Artistic Appropriation

George Jacobs has been lucky enough to have shared his life with a variety of fluffy friends, and currently lives with his pet degus, Abby and Lilly. He enjoys spending his time hiking, painting, reading, and playing board games. By night he is a writer of short and fantastical stories, by day he works with trains. For more information and other stories, please visit his site: https://georgejacobsauthor.wordpress.com/

E.C. Bell
What Frisky Wrought When the Wheels Fell Off the World

E.C. Bell is the author of the award-winning paranormal Marie Jenner Mystery series. She lives in Alberta, Canada, and when she's not writing, she's scouting out new locations for her upcoming novels or renovating her round house where she lives with her husband and their rescue dog, Buddy.

That's right. Her house is round.

Dōes The Dōg Die?

RHONDA PARRISH

"Introduction" by Rhonda Parrish—Nothing bad happens to any dogs.

"The Empress of Marshmallow" by Chadwick Ginther—A dog is put in a precarious situation but the worst thing that happens to her is that she gets wet.

"Davy Bones and the Domestication of The Dutchman" by Jennifer Lee Rossman—A dog is very lonely and sad but she does find companionship of a sort in the end.

"Johnson the Terror" by Meghan Beaudry—The dogs are all right.

"Ghost Pirate Dognapper" by Kristen Brand—A dog is dognapped but doesn't seem to mind. She is briefly frightened but gets over it quickly.

"Blackbark's Collar" by Richard Lau—Two ships full of dogs are lost to a sea monster, including two dogs being swallowed by the monster. The dog narrating the story also loses his paws off page and now uses hooks.

"Let the Water Drink First" by V.F. LeSann—Bad things happen to people, mostly off-page but with some references in the story, but the dogs are okay.

"New Tricks" by Alice Dryden—A dog is in aerial combat and crashes his plane, then later is chased and takes a big fall. But he survives it all unharmed.

"Torvi, Viking Queen" by Melanie Marttila—Two dogs fight each other and are tossed overboard during a storm, but both escape any serious harm in the end.

"Under the Curse of Jupiter" by Mathew Austin—Dogs get sick from eating chocolate. Some dogs die, though mostly off the page.

"The Boomer Bust" by JB Riley—Nothing bad happens to the dog.

"What Gold Smells Like" by Frances Pauli—A dog is bullied. Another (antagonist) dog is knocked unconscious and marooned on an island.

"Artistic Appropriation" by George Jacobs—Humans are extinct but the dogs are okay.

"What Frisky Wrought When the Wheels Fell Off the World" by E.C. Bell—One dog (probably?) dies off the page—he's definitely ganged up on in a fight—and several dogs fall into the river, but hopefully they can swim.